Why Did I Write This Book?

The answer to that question is simple: I couldn't stand back any longer and watch other young women go through the same hurt and pain that I went through, because I now know that it doesn't have to be this way.

For so long, I judged my body, I battled with my weight, I had a negative relationship with food, and I hated what ~~saw when~~ I looked in the mirror. Fast-forward to today, an~~d~~ ~~ou~~ how liberating it feels to have broken free ~~from~~ ~~.~~ I feel like a new person. I'm happy. I e~~at~~ delicious and nourishing foods, ~~n!~~ I had to hit rock bottom though, be~~~~ ~~~~here is a much better way to live.

I want to share what I've learned with all the young women out there who are struggling with negative thoughts and feelings about their bodies. It's time for change. It's time for our generation of young women to step out of the shackles of society's expectations on body image. Let's build solid foundations of self-love and self-acceptance together, and let's walk proudly into our future feeling free, confident, and empowered. My dream is that this book will give every girl who reads it the tools she needs to do just that!

A Letter to You, Gorgeous Girlie

Dear Gorgeous Girlie,

Being a teenage girl is harder than it looks, isn't it? Navigating the world of hormones, friendship dramas, parental expectations, peer pressure, relationships, and schoolwork can feel like a never-ending rollercoaster. Trust me, I feel ya! It wasn't very long ago that I was walking that rocky path, too.

However, out of all the pressures that teenage girls face every day, there is one that not enough people are talking about, yet it looms menacingly over so many young girls. It's a nasty epidemic sweeping through the corridors of our schools, following us home at night, and even creeping into our bedrooms, making us feel yucky and terrible. What is it?

It's the pressure to be perfect.

It's the thought that "I'm not good enough unless I look a certain way." It's the constant comparing of ourselves to other girls and to the "perfect-looking" models in magazines and on billboards that seem to be everywhere— and always thinking that we, somehow, fall short. Does any of this sound familiar to you?

Learning to Love the Girl in the Mirror

A Teenage Girl's Guide
To Living A Happy And Healthy Life

by
Helena Grace Donald

Torch Flame Media, LLC

In this book the author shares the self-empowering processes that enabled her to recognize and change the unhelpful judgments about her body that were causing her distress. She offers this personal information in good faith and with the heartfelt intention of empowering others. While the processes in this book can be helpful, they are not intended as a substitute for, but as a complement to, professional medical and psychological support, where appropriate.

Edited by Sylvia Cottrell
Interior design by Sara Zibrat
Cover design by Michael Sloane and Aimee Attia

ISBN 978-0-9988161-0-4
Library of Congress Control Number: 2017904430

Publisher's Cataloging-In-Publication Data
(Prepared by The Donohue Group, Inc.)

Names: Donald, Helena Grace.
Title: Learning to love the girl in the mirror : a teenage girl's guide to living a
    happy and healthy life / by Helena Grace Donald.
Description: Los Angeles, CA : Torch Flame Media, LLC, [2017] | Interest age
    level: 012-021. | Includes bibliographical references.
Identifiers: LCCN 2017904430 | ISBN 978-0-9988161-0-4 | ISBN
    978-0-9988161-1-1 (ebook)
Subjects: LCSH: Self-esteem in adolescence. | Self-esteem in young adults. |
    Teenage girls--Conduct of life. | Young women--Conduct of life. | Crit-
    icism, Personal. | Body image in girls. | Body image in women. | Eating
    disorders in adolescence.
Classification: LCC BF724.3.S36 D66 2017 (print) | LCC BF724.3.S36 (ebook) |
    DDC 155.5/182--dc23

Torch Flame Media, LLC
Los Angeles, CA
USA

Table of Contents

Let me ask you:

- ♥ Are you happy with the skin you're in?
- ♥ Have you ever been on a diet?
- ♥ Do you have a secret?

I had a secret. A big one. I hid the fact that I was so unhappy with my own body after going on countless diets that I started to voluntarily throw up my meals and starve myself. Pretty extreme, huh? Pretty rare? Sadly, no. Millions of girls around the world wake up every morning and hate what they see in the mirror, and over 50% of teenage girls use unhealthy behaviors to control their weight.[1]

What's worse is that we don't talk about it because we're ashamed. We think we're the only ones who feel this way. But let me reassure you, if you are feeling insecure about how you look or if you are struggling with unhealthy eating habits (or both), you are definitely not alone. Let's be really clear about that from the get-go.

You are not alone.

Of course, not all teenage girls develop full-fledged eating disorders, but every calorie-count or new fad diet can be the seed of one. The constant pressure to be "perfect" and to "fit in" can easily lead to unhealthy and,

---

1   Heather R. Gallivan, PsyD, LP, "Teens, Social Media And Body Image." Park Nicollet Melrose Center. Web. Accessed October 14, 2016. http://www. macmh.org/wp-content/uploads/2014/05/18_ Gallivan_Teens-social-media-body-image-presentation-H-Gallivan-Spring-2014.pdf.

yes, sometimes harmful habits around food. This is a road you really do not want to take. It leads to nothing but sadness, pain, and misery. I know because I've been down that road, and I want to tell you that it absolutely does not have to be this way.

This book is my brutally honest story of how I managed to kick an eating disorder in the butt and, in the process, discovered a whole new healthier way of thinking, feeling, and behaving that has made me love and appreciate the skin I'm in. I'm going to share with you everything I discovered on my journey from hating my body to really loving the girl in the mirror, and I will do it with as much love and honesty as I can possibly pack into these pages, because...

Every girl deserves to feel happy and comfortable in the skin that she's in.

Whether you're already struggling with an eating disorder or you're just trying to navigate your way through all the various pressures that come with being a teenager, this book can be your personal guide to having a great relationship with yourself and your body for the rest of your life.

It doesn't matter where you're starting from—you can learn to have a healthy, positive, and loving relationship with yourself and your body at any point. If I could do it, you can do it too. If you decide to take this journey with me and follow the easy steps laid out for you in this book,

I promise you that one day soon, you too will wake up, look in the mirror, and beam with happiness at the girl looking back at you.

Love, joy & inspiration,

Helena xoxo

To have the body you love, you must start by loving the body you have.

—Mel Wells

CHAPTER 1

Say Goodbye to Little Miss Critical

In this chapter, you will:

♥ Discover exactly who has been knocking your self-confidence and making you feel bad about yourself.

♥ Learn how to say bye-bye to the meanest bully you'll ever meet (and feel great about it!)

Do you have a Little Miss Critical in your life? I bet you do. We *all* do! Does yours just visit from time to time, or has she moved in permanently? Mine used to pop in occasionally in my early teens, but as the pressures of teenage life increased, her visits became more and more frequent until, finally, when I was about 16, she stuck to me like glue and wouldn't leave. Little Miss Critical came everywhere with me.

Every morning she was there, waiting for me at the bathroom mirror:

"You've got another disgusting, humongous spot on your chin!"

She would stand right next to me, criticizing my reflection in the bedroom mirror as I got dressed:

"That skirt is waaay too tight! You've put on weight again!"

She was with me at school, comparing me negatively to other girls she thought were slimmer or smarter or more social than I was:

"How come Emily can have a perfect figure and you can't?"

And she was there at every mealtime, whispering threats in my ear about the weight I might put on if I ate what was on my plate:

"That pizza has a gazillion calories. If you eat that, you'll be a big fat pig!"

She thought her job was to make me and my life "perfect," and she tried to do it by pointing out all the ways I fell far short of "perfection." One of her favorite things to do was to scrutinize my body, looking for flaws. She would squeeze my tummy and pinch any fat she could find, making tears well up in my eyes. When I walked, she would hold an imaginary mirror behind me to make me conscious of the size of my butt, the way my thighs rubbed together, and the cellulite she said was beginning to appear on the backs of my legs. Her sarcastic and hurtful comments echoed in my head, telling me that I was not good enough the way I was and that I would never be successful at what I wanted to do until I was skinnier.

Because of her, I put more and more pressure on myself to be the perfect size, the perfect student—the perfect everything. I tried weight-loss plans, diets, detoxes, and I even fantasized about having cosmetic surgery to slim my hips and thighs when I would be older. As far as Little Miss Critical was concerned, I would only be good enough when I had a "perfect" body, perfect grades, and a perfect life. The more powerful she became, the unhealthier my obsession with my weight became.

Eventually, I reached a tipping point when I felt like the only way I could cope with her constant criticism and put-downs was either to starve myself or throw up my meals. In the end I did both—often in the same day. Looking back, I can see that I was really struggling to gain some control over my life and my body while simultaneously maintaining my image of having it all together. Some days I would try to see how long I could push myself without eating, then I would feel so hungry and anxious that I would stuff myself with food in an attempt to numb the pain and anxiety I was feeling. I'd do this until my stomach was about to explode—and then I'd emotionally release it all by throwing up.

I hid this behavior from everyone. It was my shameful secret. I used to excuse myself from the family dinner table, run the bathroom taps so that nobody would hear me, throw up whatever I'd eaten, and then return to the table as if nothing had happened. I counted calories throughout the day, and Little Miss Critical always had something to say about everything I ate. Don't get me started on how harsh she could be if I ate anything that she perceived to be indulgent! One birthday, she even refused to let me eat a slice of my own birthday cake.

Sometimes, Little Miss Critical would join in with my friends'

Little Miss Criticals, and they would all enjoy a full-on "let's put ourselves down!" group session. You know how these sessions go, right? One girl points out a flaw she thinks she has, such as a spot on her face, and then another girl joins in by saying that she feels fat and bloated, which leads someone else to comment on how she has put on so much weight that her jeans won't zip up. It becomes a kind of competition to see who can find the most negative thing to say about themselves.

Do you recognize any of this from your own life? Have you and your friends ever taken part in these kinds of sessions?

Seriously, why do we do this to ourselves? Is it because we feel that by pointing out our "flaws" we're bonding with each other? Or do we maybe do it because we're hoping our friends will say "don't be silly, you look great!" and boost our confidence? Or are we just hoping that if other girls point out their imperfections, then maybe we won't feel so alone with ours? Or is it simply because we're programmed by society to think that other people won't like us if we think highly of ourselves, so we go in the opposite direction and criticize ourselves instead? I think most of us probably do it for all of these reasons at different times— however, there is one thing I'm absolutely sure of, and that is:

Not a single one of those reasons is good enough to justify the harm we are doing to ourselves and to others when we do it!

Let me ask you a very serious question: Would you want to hang out with a friend who was constantly judging you, criticizing you, and putting you down? Seriously, would you? I doubt it. You'd be straight out the door! And yet many of us wake up with, spend our days with, and go to bed with such a person! Our very own Little Miss Critical.

I allowed my Little Miss Critical to have way too much power in my life and, because of that, I was really horrible to my body: criticizing it, starving it, overfeeding it, and making it sick. But, unlike a friend who could just walk away and stop being friends with me, my poor body had to stick around and put up with all the abuse.

Do you think my body just took all that abuse without fighting back? Absolutely not! It chose the perfect way to make me pay for my meanness—it gained weight and refused to let go of it, no matter what I did, until I started to treat it with the kindness and respect it deserved.

I had to learn the hard way that constant self-criticism and unhealthy dieting were never going to get me to where I wanted to be. The only place these things lead to is Misery Street. I know that street well because I lived there for a few years and, believe me, it's definitely not a desirable address.

Between the ages of 16 and 19, my Little Miss Critical worked her butt off trying to make me skinny enough to be the "perfect" size, but despite all my dieting, detoxing, and punishing gym workouts, I just kept getting bigger. And, the bigger I got, the more Little Miss Critical did her thing. Until, one day I looked at the girl in the mirror, with tears streaming down my face, and I knew that I simply couldn't go on living like this. Misery Street had become unbearable.

I had tried everything to lose weight, but nothing was working. I was the heaviest I had ever been and the most demoralized and depressed I had ever been. I couldn't go on feeling this way about myself any longer; I had reached my rock bottom and it felt dangerous. That's when I made the decision that changed my life. I have to be honest and say that it wasn't an easy decision to make. In fact, it was really scary. But I knew, at that moment, that I had to make it.

Either I was going to go on tormenting myself for the rest of my life, fighting a losing battle to make my body conform to some "'ideal shape" that it obviously wasn't designed to be. Or, I was going to have to stop everything I'd been doing—the dieting, detoxing, bingeing, purging, and body hating—and try my hardest to accept my body the way it was—totally, and without conditions.

Not if I lost weight.

Not if my thighs got smaller.

Not if my boobs were magically two sizes bigger.

Not at some imaginary time in the future when everything would be "perfect."

No, I had to start accepting myself exactly as I was right then. I couldn't continue battling with the girl in the mirror. I was too exhausted from the fight.

I decided that if I was ever going to get out of Misery Street, Little Miss Critical would have to go. But how was I going to get rid of her? She'd been with me for so long, and she had no intention of just packing her bags and leaving. No way! Once I'd decided to say goodbye to her, she tried every trick in the book to persuade me that I needed her. She tried to make me doubt myself and my decision.

"But, if you don't have me to tell you what's wrong with you, you'll never be perfect!"

Sometimes, when I felt strong, I would just tell her to go take a hike and she would leave me in peace for a while. But, like all bullies, she could sniff out weakness from a distance, so anytime I felt vulnerable or stressed (which was quite often in those early days), she would come back with a vengeance to remind me how "not good enough" I was. It was an ongoing battle; whenever I seemed to be gaining ground, she'd outwit me by slipping in where my defenses were weakest and retaking her position of power over me, which would leave me feeling anxious, confused and tearful.

"You can eat that if you want to, but you do know your thighs are getting bigger, don't you?"

That battle went on for months, and there were times when I thought I'd never escape from the hold she had over me. Then, in answer to a heartfelt prayer, help began to appear from different sources. To begin with, it came in the form of a great little technique that I discovered on YouTube.[2] This technique helped me to disempower Little Miss Critical by literally getting her out of my head. And, then I met three incredibly caring and helpful new friends called *Kindness*, *Positivity*, and *Gratitude*.

The support of these amazing new friends empowered me in my battle with Little Miss C. The more I hung out with them, the stronger and happier I became. They encouraged me to focus on positive things about myself that I had never paid any attention to before. They helped me to change the way I thought about myself, and I started to go from negative, judgmental, and

---

2   I'll share this technique with you later in the chapter

critical to kind, appreciative, and respectful. They taught me to treat myself the way I would treat an actual best friend and, at their suggestion, I came up with a new motto:

If you wouldn't say it to your best friend, don't say it to yourself.

I have been living by that motto for the last three years, and the difference it has made in my life makes me want to cry with happiness even now! The whole energy inside my head has changed from negative and miserable to positive and upbeat. Now, Little Miss Critical finds it really hard to gain entry to the best party in town—my life. She just doesn't fit in with my crowd anymore.

And, I'm happy to say that none of Little Miss C's threats about how disastrous my life would be, without her to keep me on track, turned out to be true. In fact, when she left, everything in my life started to get better:

- 😃 I stopped criticizing my body and trying to change it, which lifted a whole load of stress off my shoulders.

- 😃 I focused on accepting and appreciating myself just as I was, which made me (and my body) feel a whole lot happier.

- 😃 I got rid of the bathroom scales that used to measure my self-worth. Bye-bye to beating myself up most mornings.

- 😃 I stopped dieting, started to eat regular meals, and fell in love with food again

☺ I discovered how to gain control over the urge to binge[3] and purge[4] and I have been free from bulimia ever since.

☺ Over time, the excess weight that my body had been holding onto began to naturally melt away.

☺ My relationship with my mother, which had been deteriorating rapidly, got better.

☺ I went from feeling like a victim of my own and other people's expectations to feeling free, confident, empowered and happy in the skin I'm in.

It didn't happen overnight. Learning to love the girl in the mirror has been a journey with challenges, ups and downs, and occasional bumps in the road. But oh, my goodness! It's been exciting and definitely worth taking!

I've discovered a whole new way of thinking, speaking, feeling and behaving that has turned my world the right way up. I want to share it with you, so that you can avoid going anywhere near Misery Street. And, if you're already there, I hope that each chapter in this book will shine a light to illuminate your path back to where we all deserve to live–"Happy To Be Me Street."

The first step involves getting to know your own Little Miss Critical and seeing how she has been affecting your life so far

Are you ready to do that? Great! Let's go...

---

3 See Chapter 5
4 See Chapter 7

Big Sis Memo

If you begin to feel emotional while taking this first step, I want you to know that that is perfectly normal. The things that Little Miss Critical says to us are often upsetting and hurtful, so if you feel vulnerable, I want you to remember that you are not alone. There are so many of us in this together. In my heart, I am with you every step of the way, energetically holding your hand.

However, if you feel that you need some personal support while taking this step, or any of the other steps in this book, I recommend confiding in a parent, or in another adult that you trust. You might choose to have someone in the room with you while you are doing the exercise or, alternatively, you might prefer to just tell them that you are doing it and ask them to be nearby afterwards if you want to talk to them, or if you just want a big loving hug. Choose whatever feels right for you. I believe in you, girl. You can do this.

Identify Your Own Little Miss Critical

Get yourself a pen and a notebook, and go to a private place where you won't be disturbed. When you're ready, write down your answers to the following questions.

1. What does Little Miss Critical say to you that makes you feel bad? (Notice and record all the harsh criticisms that come into your head, no matter how mean or ugly they might be.)

2. Does she ever compare you negatively to your friends/other girls at school/movie stars/models in magazines? How often? What kinds of things does she say?

3. Does she ever make comments about what you eat? If so, what does she say?

4. Does she ever point out your "imperfections" in front of other people? Can you remember some of the things she said?

5. How does it make you feel about yourself when she puts you down or shames you? (for example: stressed/ miserable/depressed/angry/not good enough/guilty/ other)

6. When she criticizes you or puts you down, does her voice sound like your own voice in your head or like somebody else's voice? A parent/teacher/sibling/bully at school/character on TV, for example?

Well done!

That was very brave, and I am so proud of your courage. It was important to do that so that you could get to know your own Little Miss Critical and see for yourself just how much power she has had over you up until now. But don't worry—we're going to ask her to leave soon.

But before we do that, I'm going to suggest something that may sound crazy. What if you took a moment to actually thank Little Miss Critical for all that she's done for you? "What? Thank her!? Why on earth would I do that?" I hear you say. I know, I know. After uncovering all the negative ways she has affected your life, that's probably the last thing you want to do. But there's a really empowering reason why I'm asking you to do this.

You see, Little Miss Critical is actually a part of you.

She wasn't always a part of you. She wasn't a part of you when you were born. She probably wasn't a part of you when you were a toddler or even a little girl, but somewhere along the way as you were growing up she popped into your life. It might have been when you sensed that someone disapproved of the way you looked or the way you behaved. Maybe you were told off or criticized by a parent or a teacher and you felt embarrassed or shamed. Maybe another child made hurtful remarks or judged or excluded you for some reason.

Things like this happen to all of us at times when we're growing up, and it can feel pretty devastating to our young selves. The truth is that we all really just want to be liked and approved of; we all want to be accepted, and we will do everything in our power to make sure that we are. That's where Little Miss Critical comes in.

At some point during our childhood, this little gremlin develops in our personality to protect us from the disapproval of other people. Yep, I said, "protect." She takes on the role of keeping us safe by making us "acceptable," and the only way she knows how to do this is to point out all the things that other people might not like about us or might not find "acceptable."

She wants us to be happy, so she becomes the internalized voice of all the people whose approval we seek, such as our parents, our friends, the popular kids at school, the bullies, boys, girls, society as a whole...phew! That's why my Little Miss Critical was working her butt off trying to make me "perfect." She was afraid that I would not be acceptable to the people whose approval mattered to me unless I conformed to some idealized notion of the perfect daughter, the perfect student, the perfect size, perfect blah blah blah! Of course, that wasn't true, but she believed it was, and she did her job so well that she also convinced me that it was true.

When I realized all this, it made me feel differently about her. It actually made me feel kind of grateful to her. So, before I asked her to leave, I felt that it was important to thank her for all her hard work on my behalf. What she had done was definitely misguided and it caused me a lot of stress and pain, but her intentions had been good. She'd been trying to protect me from the pain she thought I would suffer if other people disapproved of me and rejected me.

Her childish thinking was:

"If I criticize her and point out all the things that are 'wrong' with her, then she'll work hard to be 'perfect,' and then she'll 'fit in' to other people's idea of what is 'acceptable,' and then she'll be happy!"

But it didn't work out the way Little Miss C thought it would. Far from making me perfect or happy, it just made me feel terrible about myself. You see, Little Miss Critical is not a mature, wise, or enlightened part of us; she doesn't have the ability to see the bigger picture. Her idea of what's good for us was formulated when we were children and, although *we've* gotten older and more mature, *she* still has the immature, magical thinking of a child:

"Maybe if I'm good and I do everything that everybody wants me to do and I look the way my parents, or peers, or boys, or even fashion magazine editors think I should look, maybe then everybody will like me and approve of me and I'll be accepted!"

She disguises her immaturity behind a critical and judgmental mask, and she does it so well that she fools some people for their whole lives.

Don't let her mask fool you.

When we expose Little Miss Critical for what she really is, we disempower her. She behaves like a mean bully, but she's just an immature and misguided part of us who takes her role as our protector so seriously that she will do whatever she thinks it takes, regardless of the consequences. You now have to take the power back from her and tell her who's boss in your life. (Yeah, that would be you!)

Thank Little Miss Critical and Tell Her to Pack Her Bags!

It's time to lovingly but firmly tell Little Miss C to pack up her bags and go. One of the best ways to do this is by writing her a goodbye letter. Okay...so it might seem a little strange to write a goodbye letter to an imaginary part of yourself, but seriously, it helps! It can be so therapeutic to get out onto the page all the thoughts and feelings you've been bottling up. Plus, it helps Little Miss Critical to understand why she has to go. So grab a pen and paper and allow your thoughts to spill out onto the page. Take as long as you need and say all that you need to say.

My goodbye letter to Little Miss Critical started a little like this...

Dear Little Miss Critical,

Thank you for looking out for me by trying to make me all "perfect" and everything. I know you were doing your best and I appreciate how hard you've worked, but <u>I want to be my own person from now on. You see, I no longer want to be anyone else's idea of perfect,</u> so I don't need you to tell me what to do or how to feel, because I'm way stronger than you realize and I can look out for myself now.

Explain to her that you've decided to accept and love yourself just the way you are. Tell her that you appreciate how hard she's worked for you over the years and you know that her intentions were good, but that actually what she was doing made you very unhappy and you don't want to go on feeling that way. Tell her that you are now giving her permission to go on a long, well-deserved vacation.

Now, remember that Little Miss Critical takes her job very seriously, so she's probably not going to be very happy about just being told she's no longer wanted. She's probably going to try to hold on to her position of power over you. This is where the fun technique I mentioned earlier comes in. It will help you to disempower Little Miss Critical and get her out of your head.

Are you ready to do that?

Let's make it happen...

Get Little Miss C Out of Your Head!

♥ Look over the list you made of all the hurtful things Little Miss Critical has said to you.

♥ Imagine you can hear her saying the first critical thing on your list, but instead of the normal voice she uses, change the voice in your head and make it sound really silly and funny. You could make it high-pitched and squeaky and speed it up like a crazy cartoon character, or maybe give it a really funny accent that will make you want to laugh. Make it as silly as you can!

♥ Now, hold both of your hands out in front of you with your thumbs pointing upwards and imagine that you are floating the silly voice out of your head and into your thumbs.

♥ Wiggle your thumbs around like puppets and imagine that you are hearing the critical comment coming from the silly voice at the tip of your wiggling thumbs. Have fun with this!

♥ Keep on doing this until you cannot take the critical comment seriously anymore and it has no power over you.

♥ Now, move on to the next hurtful remark on your list and do the same thing. In your own time, work your way through the list until you cannot take any of the things Little Miss Critical says to you seriously.

♥ Do this exercise any time LMC tries to get back in your head again.

Chapter Summary

In this chapter, you have:

♥ Become aware of the existence of your own Little Miss Critical and the power she has had in your life up until now

♥ Come to know that she is the voice of other people's expectations and prejudices (your parents, teachers, friends, society) and she thinks it is her job to criticize you to make you "acceptable."

♥ Written her a "thank you and goodbye" letter.

♥ Developed a technique you can use to get her out of your head and disempower her.

Well done. You go, girl! You have taken the first step on your journey towards loving the girl in the mirror. Be proud of yourself. I'm proud of you.

Perfection is the disease of a nation...

—Beyoncé, "Pretty Hurts"

CHAPTER 2

Step Out of the Perfection Complex

In this chapter, we're going to:

* Throw the doors wide open and expose the whole myth of perfection.

* Discover the powerful influence that media and advertising have on how we think and feel.

* Understand that perfection doesn't really exist.

You don't want to be a Jell-O mold, do you?

Have you ever made Jell-O? (Or, for my British readers, jelly?) To make Jell-O, you have to pour hot liquid into a mold so that, when it sets, it'll hold a specific shape. I look at the so-called "ideal body shapes" that so many people strive for today as Jell-O molds that we're all trying to set ourselves into. Can you imagine what it would be like if every female on the planet was made from the same mold? There would be nothing unique about any of us.

Instead of an abundant variety of shapes, colors, and personalities, the world would be filled with identical, wibbly-wobbly jelly blobs. How boring would that be? But, as well as being boring, it's also completely unachievable! The "ideal" body shape that many girls try to fit themselves into is changing all the time. It changes from decade to decade.

What we think is attractive now definitely wasn't the way girls and women wanted to look even just a few years ago, and probably won't be the way they want to look in a few years' time. As I write this book, big bottoms are in, but if fashion follows the trend of the last 100 years,[5] they will not be in for long. In just one century, the number of different "ideal" female shapes there have been is really hilarious. Let's take a look back through the decades and see:

1910s: small bust and waist, big hips

1920s: straight up and down, no curves

1930s: curvy top and bottom

1940s: tall, angular, no curves, broad shoulders, long legs

1950s: petite, curvy, hourglass shape

1960s: beanpole skinny, no curves

1970s: long, lean, slight curves

1980s: tall, athletic, muscular

1990s: small, slim-framed, gaunt

2000s: athletic, muscular, visible abs

2010s: curves, big bottoms!

Seriously, how is anyone meant to keep up with that? It's completely subjective and constantly changing. What's in one

---

5   See http://greatist.com/grow/100-years-womens-body-image

minute is out the next, and that's largely controlled by fashion editors sitting around a table deciding on the next trend to put on the front cover of their magazines.

We are bombarded with these images of so-called "perfection" every day—not only in magazines, but also on TV, on our social media sites, and peering down at us from massive billboards. And, it's so easy to feel insecure and "not good enough" in comparison. But, we don't have to allow it to influence us. We have a choice.

Recently, I was sitting down to watch one of my favorite shows when a commercial came on, showing a "perfect-looking" model in a bikini running in slow motion along a white sandy beach. For a split second, I felt a pang of jealousy. Luckily, my moment of jealous insecurity was short-lived; I quickly flipped a switch in my brain and said:

"Stop!" Why should I let a commercial on television have the power to make me feel insecure about myself?"

I then gave myself a gentle pep-talk. I told myself that I don't need to look like anyone else, or be like anyone else, to be acceptable. I reassured myself that I am perfectly imperfect and that I accept and appreciate myself exactly as I am.

It felt really empowering to know that I can choose how I want to feel, rather than have that dictated to me by anything or anyone outside of myself, such as a random advertisement on TV that was trying to sell me something.

Would this always have been the case? No! Not so long ago, I would have got stuck in pure jealousy and resentment. I would have beaten myself up because my body did not look like the model in the commercial.

How come she can have slim hips, slim thighs and still have boobs!? It's just not fair!

But, luckily, as part of my healing journey, I trained myself to quit the insane, confidence-destroying habit of comparing myself to other girls. There is absolutely nothing good to be gained from it. As well as giving us a negative self-image, it also turns us into victims. Why? Because we are allowing our self-worth to be determined by other people's unrealistic expectations of perfection.

Who gives anybody the power to decide what is good, better or best when it comes to women's bodies?

The answer to that question is, *we* do. And our mothers do, and our aunties and our grandmothers and every woman who has ever bought into the myth that her body, or your body, or any other female body is not good enough because it does not conform to somebody else's idea of perfection.

My mother, whom I love and respect very much, used to be a victim of that disempowering mentality until she realized how dangerous and wrong it was. She, like so many other women, had been sucked into the myth that girls and women need to look a certain way to be accepted. Her misguided belief added majorly to the Little Miss Critical voice in my head that caused me to hate my own body. For me, telling Little Miss Critical to pack her bags and leave coincided with telling my own mother that

I was rejecting her opinion about my body. It was something I needed to do for my own survival. She had my best interests at heart, as most mothers do, but her constant concern about my weight was contributing to me not accepting myself as I was, and was also a huge source of tension in our relationship. I knew that I needed to stop looking for her approval, or anybody else's approval, and accept myself regardless of what anybody else thought. That was the only way I could heal.

Another thing that really helped me in my recovery from body-hating was to look at advertising from a different perspective. Rather than just take it at face value, I began to analyze how and why it works. That really helped me to see things more clearly and helped me to step out of the "perfection complex."

Let me take you through a potential behind-the-scenes scenario of what happens before you pick up a magazine, or turn on your screen and see yet another half-naked sexy young model lying on the beach advertising some brand of makeup or diet drink or whatever.

Just for the sake of being neutral and not targeting any specific product, I'm going to make up a random drink called "Peachy."

A beverage company has created a new zero-calorie drink called "Peachy" and it's time to market it.

Because it's a zero-calorie drink, they are going to target the marketing at people interested in keeping fit and managing their weight.

The marketing experts know that a great way to entice people to buy something is to first make them feel insecure and then offer them a solution to their perceived problem. [6]

They create an advertising campaign that shows a young, "perfect-looking" model running on the beach—this will bring out our comparison insecurities as intended—and then they follow it by a close-up of her "peachy" bottom as she turns to the camera and winks.

Expert photoshoppers will contour and color the model's bottom to make it look like a peach, and also to match the color of the can.

A young woman sees this image on a billboard and thinks, "Gosh, wouldn't life be like a walk on the beach if I had her butt?

The next time this young woman goes to buy a drink to quench her thirst, she sees the same peach-colored can in the

---

6 Theodysseyonline.com

cooler and remembers the beautiful model's butt. She picks that drink over all the others because (subconsciously) she believes that if she drinks it, maybe she'll be one step closer to looking like that girl in the ad.

Result: The beverage company makes millions of dollars of profits all around the world! Mission accomplished.

The whole point of advertising is to persuade us that if we buy a certain product, we will have the chance of looking like, or feeling like, the person in the advertisement. And everything about the ad, whether it is on our television screens, on a billboard, or on social media, is designed to appeal to all of our senses—to make us feel that we really want or need that product. But, if you look behind the final picture that is portrayed, you will begin to notice the deliberate planning and skill that goes into creating these images of "perfection." You will see that they are cleverly crafted to evoke a desire in us to have that product or that lifestyle. And, in many cases, it is total illusion.

To begin with, the "perfect-looking" models and celebrities that you see on billboards, in magazines and on social media don't just wake up in the morning looking like that. They have personal trainers who put them through rigorous body workouts once, sometimes twice, a day. Many also have personal nutritionists, makeup artists, fashion stylists, hairstylists, endless beauty treatments and some even have had cosmetic surgery. That is all before they've even stepped in front of the camera! Then comes the special flattering lighting and the magic of retouching, which can completely alter how somebody looks so that they appear, well, perfect.

On top of that, models and celebrities know how to pose in a way that shows them off to their best advantage. They know which side of their face to present to the camera; how to sit and stand to make their legs look longer and slimmer; and how to position their arms, legs, hips and shoulders to give them a more flattering silhouette. They have learned the tricks of their trade, because their careers require them to look good and to present themselves in the most flattering light. It's their job.

It is also important to note that most of these "perfect-looking" girls and women are no longer teenagers; they have left the acne, braces and body changes of adolescence behind. So, for any teenage girl to compare herself, as she is in her natural state when she wakes up in the morning, with this level of sophisticated trickery is a totally unfair and confidence-destroying comparison.

And, believe it or not, many of these gorgeous-looking models also have body hang-ups just like the rest of the female population. Recently, after reading a first draft of this book, a model friend of mine called me from a photoshoot to tell me that all the other models were complaining about some part of their bodies and comparing themselves negatively to one another. Having just become aware of her own Little Miss Critical, it made my friend so sad to see that none of these models felt happy with their body the way it was. And these are some of the icons of "perfection" that we aspire to look like!

The sad truth is that negative body image issues affect girls and women of all shapes and sizes. It's not about how we look on the outside; it is about how we feel about ourselves on the inside and, sadly, that is being dictated by the photoshopped images and expectations of perfection that are being fed to us by the media, and by everyone who buys into the myth. We have become enslaved to an idea of perfection that doesn't exist in the real world and it is making us feel "not good enough," stressed and unhappy. It is robbing us of our inner power and preventing us from living a life of freedom and joy. And, worst of all, it is causing too many of us to have eating disorders and mental health issues.

And, it's not just body comparisons that can cause us to feel insecure. It's also social and lifestyle comparisons. There's a huge pressure, especially in the teenage years, to appear to be popular, to have a perfect social life, to be constantly surrounded by cool friends, doing exciting things, and to post evidence of all this on social media for others to see. And, for many, if not most of us, this is not always how our lives are, nor should it have to be.

It's important to remember that most people only post the idealized version of their lives—the image they want other people to see. It can be so easy to mistake these "perfect-looking," filtered images for reality. We compare other people's "highlights" with our "everyday" and end up feeling "boring" and "not good enough" in comparison to them.

As a young teenager, when I saw photos of classmates out socializing, looking like they were having the most exciting time, I felt excluded and insignificant because I wasn't there and that was not my life. And, I can also remember times when I was on the other side of that kind of scenario. I remember a sleepover when I was about fourteen where we were all tired and a bit hormonal and not really having much fun. Suddenly it started to snow and somebody suggested that we go outside and make snow angels. Immediately, phones started clicking and soon photos of us playing in the snow, laughing our heads off and looking like we were having a magical time, appeared on Facebook. Anyone who saw those photos probably thought that they had missed out on a perfectly fabulous party. But, was that the reality? No! The photos only showed a small snapshot, not the wider view.

The reality is that photos, whether they're selfies or taken by a professional photographer, don't always tell the whole story. In some cases, they present a totally false impression. Just because you see a picture that portrays an exciting or perfect life does not mean the people in the photo feel happy. So, please don't allow yourself to fall into the trap of thinking that perfection or happiness exist somewhere out there where the grass is greener than where you are right now. If even top models, who are often looked up to as icons of perfection, are not happy with how they look, what on earth are we all striving for?

The big lesson I have learned on my journey is that it's not possible to find true or lasting happiness outside of yourself until you first make peace with who you are on the inside. Happiness is an inside job. It comes from the inside out, not the other way around.

We do not need to look like anyone else, be a certain size or shape, or belong to a particular social group, in order to feel beautiful and happy.

We need to accept and celebrate our own uniqueness and choose to be happy in the skin we're in.

Every single one of us is a unique human being with talents and gifts to share with the world. And if we get caught up in the superficiality of striving to fit ourselves into somebody else's idea of "perfection" we lose touch with the most beautiful and valuable part of ourselves—that part that makes us truly shine— our authentic self.

Watch Out For The Perfection Illusion

♥ As you go about your normal day-to-day routine, begin to notice how many images of "perfection" you are bombarded with on a daily basis. We've become so immune to these images that we often don't even realize what an effect they are having on our subconscious. Try counting how many you see in one day—in magazines, on billboards, on TV and on social media.

♥ See if you can notice the tricks used by models and celebrities to show themselves off to their best advantage. Are they posing in a way to draw attention to certain parts of their bodies? Notice how they place their arms. What effect does that have on their silhouette?

♥ If it is a commercial photo used to advertise something, study the effects of make-up on the image. Has the model's face been contoured to highlight her cheekbones and jaw? Have her lips been made to look fuller by extending lipstick beyond her natural lip line? Study how her eyes have been made to look bigger and brighter with eye make-up. Imagine what that model looks like with no make-up. Would the effect be the same?

♥ Do you think these photos have been photoshopped? How?

♥ To get an idea of how photos can be altered beyond recognition, see "Time Lapse Video Shows Model's Photoshop Transformation" on YouTube and prepare to be amazed!

♥ Don't let manipulated images make you think any less of yourself. Perfection is an illusion.

Your authenticity is what makes you shine!

Chapter Summary

In this chapter, you have:

♥ Discovered that the so-called "ideal" shape and size of the female body is completely subjective and constantly changing.

♥ Come to realize that your self-worth does not have to be dictated by other people's expectations about your size, shape or social life.

♥ Explored the power of media and advertising to make us feel inadequate and how we can choose not to let it.

♥ Learned that nobody else has the right to dictate how you, or any other girl or woman, should look.

♥ Discovered that "perfection" is a myth and you don't have to buy into it.

♥ Become aware that the images of a perfect life that many people post on social media can be misleading.

Well done! Now that we've examined some of the messages that society projects about beauty and perfection and how they influence our self-worth, it's time to turn the spotlight back our way and explore some of the things we can do to make us feel a lot better about ourselves.

I think happiness is what makes you pretty. Period. Happy people are beautiful. They become like a mirror and they reflect happiness.
—Drew Barrymore

CHAPTER 3

Mind Your Language!

In this chapter, we're going to look at how you can:

- ♥ **Keep Little Miss Critical from gate-crashing your party again.**

- ♥ **Lift your spirits and feel tons more optimistic every day by simply changing the words you use.**

- ♥ **Be a powerful role model for others and raise up the energy levels in your friendship group.**

Now that you know that it is pointless to waste your energy on trying to fit into a media- and advertising-dictated "perfect" mold, would you like to discover a way to become the best version of yourself? I hope your answer is yes, because that's exactly what we're going to do in this chapter! In Chapter One, we talked about the importance of saying goodbye to Little Miss Critical and getting her out of your head. Now, let's look at how you can change your energy to keep her from sneaking back in again.

Imagine that you have to move to a foreign country and you haven't learned to speak the language yet. On your first day at school, you discover that there are some kids there who can speak your language. Would you want to hang out with them, or with the kids who don't understand you or speak your language? That's a bit of a no-brainer, isn't it?

Most of us feel more comfortable communicating with people who speak the same language as we do just because it's easier. Similarly, if you don't want Little Miss Critical hovering around trying to get back inside your head again, how about changing the language that's spoken in there to one that she doesn't understand? This is where my friends, Kindness, Positivity, and Gratitude can help. (Oh, and don't worry, they're not exclusively my friends – I'm more than happy to share them with you!) You see, they speak a completely different language from Little Miss Critical. See for yourself:

LMC:	Kindness, Positivity, and Gratitude:
Harsh	Kind
Negative	Positive
Judgmental	Compassionate
Sarcastic	Supportive
Rejecting	Accepting
Belittling	Appreciative
Bullying	Friendly
Snide	Loving
Blaming	Forgiving

Can you see how these two different ways of speaking are like oil and water? They just don't mix. To keep Little Miss Critical from gatecrashing your party, change the language you speak to one that she doesn't understand.

What if you started a whole new way of speaking that is the exact opposite of Little Miss Critical's language? What if we all trained our brains to use the language of Kindness, Positivity, and Gratitude? When I started using this new way of speaking, I saw some massive shifts in how I felt almost immediately. When you do this, I promise you that your life will change for the better in ways that you can't even imagine right now.

Your words are very powerful; they can help you or hurt you, and guess who gets to choose which one it's going to be? You do!

Most of the time, we walk around thinking we have no choice in how we feel when in reality we have a lot of choice in the matter. You see, the things we say to ourselves and about ourselves can make us feel good or make us feel bad. The way we feel influences the way we behave. The way we behave teaches others how to behave towards us. The way others treat us affects how we feel. Can you see how everything is connected?

So, how do we go about changing the way we speak to ourselves? A great place to start is by becoming aware of how often we use negative language when speaking about ourselves and our lives. We are so used to putting ourselves down and moaning about our bodies and our lives that most of the time we don't even notice that we're doing it. The truth is that criticism and moaning never make anyone feel good about themselves. It just creates negative energy and makes us feel more yucky.

Try out this little experiment to see if this is true for you. Have a look at the following sentences:

"I'm sick and tired of..."

"I'm going to fail."

"I'm so stressed."

"I can't believe I ate so much food tonight. I'm so fat!"

"I'm such a loser."

"She is so much prettier than me."

"I hate my..."

"That's so boring."

"School sucks."

"I'm hopeless at..."

"That was so dumb."

"I can't believe I did that. I'm so stupid."

"That's gross."

"It's not fair."

"I have nothing to wear."

"Nothing ever goes right for me."

How do you feel after reading this list? Notice your breathing. Are you holding your breath? Does your chest feel tight? Do you find it hard to swallow? Do you feel heavy or light in your body? Does it make you feel up or down emotionally? Optimistic or pessimistic?

Now, read these sentences:

"I'm going to do my best."

"That's awesome."

"I'm so looking forward to..."

"I've been working hard, so I'm going to treat myself!"

"I'm feeling great today."

"I really enjoyed that yummy dinner."

"I love my life."

"Life loves me."

"I'm awesome."

"I'm really good at..."

"I'm so happy that..."

"I really appreciate..."

"Today's going to be a great day!"

"I had an amazing time."

"Everything looks brighter when I get a good night's sleep."

"Life is what you make it, and I'm now choosing to make mine awesome."

Did you feel differently when you read these? Notice how you're breathing. Do you feel heavier or lighter? How does your chest feel? Do you feel down or up emotionally? Pessimistic or optimistic?

When I was writing the negative list, I could feel my chest getting tight and my throat felt like it was closing, so that it became harder to swallow. My whole body tensed up. However, when I was writing the positive list, a big smile broke out on my face and I was breathing freely and easily. I felt relaxed, light, energized, and positive.

The things we think and the things we say affect how we feel.

We're all guilty of moaning and complaining from time to time, but it can become a really negative habit that pollutes our energy and the energy of all the people who have to listen it when we do it all the time. It's so contagious; all it takes is for one person in a group to start moaning and it can pollute the atmosphere with negative energy for the rest of the day.

The good news is that we can change our habits to ones that make us and the people around us feel a lot happier. I had to retrain my brain to see the positive in myself and in my life rather than always focusing on the negative. When I caught myself thinking something negative or putting myself down, I'd stop myself immediately and tell myself a positive version of the same thought. It took practice and effort, but after a fairly short while, thinking positively became a natural and healthy habit for me. Try it out for yourself and start shining!

Retrain Your Brain

1. Every time you catch yourself complaining about something, criticizing yourself, judging yourself unfairly, or being negative about yourself in any way, STOP! Then say, "delete that negative thought" and imagine it being deleted from your brain like a file from your computer.

2. Smile! Even if you don't feel like it, do it anyway. Smiling makes you feel better by releasing feel-good hormones in your body.

3. Ask yourself what would Kindness, Positivity, or Gratitude say instead. Let them help you to find something more uplifting to say—something that will make you feel better about yourself and your life instead of worse. By doing this, you are retraining your brain to think more feel-good thoughts about yourself and your life.

Simply flipping from negative to positive language can open up a whole new world of possibilities for you. Complaining may feel good for a few seconds, but the yucky energy lingers long after you have spoken the words and puts a downer on the rest of the day. If you want to feel kickass instead of kicked in the butt, it's time to start practicing the language of Kindness, Positivity, and Gratitude.

I know it can be difficult at first to find positive things to say when you start out, so I'm going to lay out some ideas for how you could flip your negative, hurtful thoughts to positive, helpful ones:

Little Miss Critical: "She is so much prettier than me."

Flip it! "She is beautiful, and her beauty doesn't take away from how awesome I am!"

Little Miss Critical: "I'll never be good enough for…"

Flip it! "I am good enough and I don't need to prove it to anyone. I am learning to love and accept myself exactly as I am, and I am grateful for all that is good in my life."

Little Miss Critical: "I'm not pretty enough to have a boyfriend or girlfriend."

Flip it! "I'm only interested in people who have depth and can see beyond superficial looks. My time is too precious to waste it on anyone who can't see how awesome I am. I am worth way more than that, and the right guy or girl will turn up for me when the time is right!"

Little Miss Critical: "I hate sports. I'm not as good as the other girls and it's so annoying."

Flip it! "Okay, so sports might not be my greatest strength, but I can still give it a go. The exercise is good for me and I'll feel better afterwards, so I'm just gonna focus on having lots of fun!"

Little Miss Critical: "Have you seen the humongous spot on my forehead? I can't leave the house."

Flip it! "No way am I gonna let something as silly as a zit dictate how I feel about myself or what I can or can't do. I'll carry it with a smile and I'm gonna have a great day!"

Little Miss Critical: "I can't do anything right. I'm such a failure."

Flip it! "I do lots of things right! I'm just having a bad day, and everybody has bad days, so it's no big deal. This feeling will pass. I'm making the decision right now to let these negative thoughts and feelings go, wipe the slate clean, and start fresh."

It's also important to remember that random critical comments you might make about yourself in front of other girls could make them feel bad about themselves, too. I remember a particular time when I was in the changing rooms at school getting ready for physical education, and one of my classmates started going on about how fat she was feeling. This girl was anything but fat, and it simply made all the other girls around her feel insecure. It felt like we were all thinking, "If *she* thinks she's fat, then that means I must be obese."

Looking back, I understand that this comment was probably coming from an insecure place within her. But nevertheless, it had a real downer effect on how the rest of us felt about ourselves.

Whenever the negative self-talk gremlin pops up within your group of friends, what can you do? Here are three options I use when it shows its mean little head around me:

Change the Subject.

If your friends start going down the path of negative self-talk, try to change the subject. Ask if anybody has seen the latest episode of *Pretty Little Liars* or the hottest new movie that has just come out. Ask about anything that you have in common, even if it's the English test you have coming up. Whatever it is that you share in common, ask about it! By doing this you are changing the group energy and, hopefully, preventing the negative gremlin from joining (and dominating) the conversation.

Nip It in the Bud!

This can be difficult and it does take confidence, but it's totally doable and will leave you feeling empowered and even better about yourself! When a close friend or family member starts talking negatively about herself around you, try saying something like: "I feel sad and uncomfortable when you say things like that about yourself, because I think you're beautiful and awesome just the way you are!" Or, try out something that will really stop them in their tracks, like: "Hey, don't talk like that about my best friend!"

I bet if somebody else was saying nasty and critical things about your best friend, you'd want to talk some sense into them at the very least. It shouldn't be any different if your friend is saying these hurtful things about herself. Sharing your feelings in a calm or fun way and without accusing the other person will help both of you. It will also probably cause the other person to re-think the way she talks about her body. Be kind and positive when you are doing this; the intention is not to make the other person feel bad, but to help her to see herself in a more positive way.

Show Them the Way!

If you feel up to it and think your friends might be receptive to this, you could choose to confront the issue in a calm, respectful way and explain why you don't want to participate in the let's-put-ourselves-down club anymore. You could explain that everyone has days where they don't feel great about their bodies, but you've noticed that everyone spends way too much energy focusing on the negatives in your group, and that you'd like to focus your energy on happier, more positive things.

If you approach this in a nice way that is not putting anyone down or making anyone feel guilty, you might get them all to agree not to participate in negative self-talk anymore. In renouncing negativity, your group of friends can find a positive way to bond over an empowering new way of behaving.

Big Sis Memo

Please remember to be kind and compassionate towards yourself and others as you practice these new habits. You are learning a new way of thinking and speaking and, like learning any new skill, it takes time for it all to come together.

Think of yourself as a little girl who is just learning to walk. You wouldn't dream of criticizing that little girl because she couldn't do it all perfectly right away, would you? You would never tell her she is stupid or that she will never get it right. In fact, you would probably praise her when she managed to take even a few baby steps. You'd be kind and encouraging towards her when she fell down. Please, please show the same kindness and patience to yourself that you would show to that little girl.

Remember that you are at the beginning of your journey. Saying goodbye to Little Miss Critical and embracing a new positive attitude towards yourself and your life is a process. It doesn't happen overnight. Allow your new friends Kindness, Positivity, and Gratitude to do their thing, and don't give any power back to Little Miss Critical by beating yourself up if she manages to sneak back in occasionally, which she probably will do from time to time when you get stressed. It still happens to me sometimes, and guess what? It's no big deal. When I fall down, I know that I can pick myself up again, give myself a big loving hug, and continue on the exciting journey of loving myself and my life. And you can do it, too. You've got this, girl!

Chapter Summary

In this chapter:

- ♥ **You have started to become aware of how powerful your thoughts and words are. Hopefully, you are also getting excited about the positive changes that are going to happen in your life when you let go of the old habit of moaning, complaining, and criticizing and embrace a more empowering way of thinking and speaking about yourself and your life.**

- ♥ **You now have a simple technique that will help you to retrain your brain to think and speak in a way that will make for a much happier, healthier, and more confident you.**

- ♥ **You are also now aware of how contagious and harmful it can be when someone brings their negative self-talk into a group, and you know a few intervention techniques that you can use when you don't want to participate in negative self-talk with others.**

How do you feel after reading this chapter? It might feel like a lot to take in, but you've got this! You are doing really well! Be proud of yourself. I'm proud of you.

Love yourself first and everything else falls in line. You really have to love yourself to get anything done in the world.

—Lucille Ball

CHAPTER 4

Best Friends Forever

In this chapter:

♥ You're going to take some very powerful steps forward by releasing any pain or hurt you may be holding onto in your body because of the things Little Miss Critical used to say and do.

♥ You're going to begin to build a strong, lifelong friendship with the girl in the mirror.

♥ You're also going to discover an easy way to step into your Supergirl power and be proud to be you!

Now that Little Miss Critical is no longer running the show and you're beginning to use the language of Kindness, Positivity, and Gratitude, you'll soon begin to notice very positive changes in the way you think and feel about yourself and your life. But I promised you more than that, and I want more than that for you. I want you to feel fabulous, unique, and special. I want you to be able to look in the mirror every day and smile at the gorgeous girl looking back at you. I want you to be able to move forward into your future feeling free, kickass confident, and empowered. Would you like that, too?

Depending on where you're at in your life right now, some of the things in this chapter may not be as relevant for you as others. For example, if you are in your early teens, then your Little Miss Critical may not have become very active or powerful yet, so the first three exercises I'm about to share with you may not be as important for you as they might be for older girls. If you feel that's the case when you read the chapter, then you can simply skip forward to the Gratitude List. What I am sharing with you here are all the steps that I, personally, went through to heal myself, but remember, I was 19 when I did this and my Little Miss Critical had already been working overtime for way too long!

I have to tell you that, for me, this was the hardest part of my journey. Why? Because it demanded a huge amount of honesty and humility. I had to face the girl in the mirror, admit what I had done to her, and apologize from the bottom of my heart and the depths of my soul for the mean way I had been treating her. It was really important for me to do this because I figured that if I wasn't willing to own up and take responsibility for what I had done, then she would never be able to really trust me again or be my friend.

When I decided to take this next step, I looked at my reflection in the mirror and, for the first time ever, I actually acknowledged the hurt and pain I had been causing myself. Then I apologized. Like, a full-on, huge, heartfelt apology. And, I'm so glad that I did, because that heartfelt apology was a whole new beginning for me; it laid the foundation for the most important relationship I will ever have: the one I have with myself.

The most important relationship you will ever have is the one you have with yourself, so treat it with respect, love, and appreciation.

Friends will come in and out of your life at different times, as will relationships and partners, but the one person who will always be with you for the rest of your life is you. So, stop for a second and ask yourself this pretty important question:

Would you rather spend the rest of your life with:

a) someone you respect, appreciate, and love—someone who trusts you and wants you to be happy, or

b) someone you cannot stand the sight of—someone who knows that you hate her and thinks that she is not good enough?

I know that, for some of you, this will be a complete no-brainer. Of course you want the first one! But I also know that, for many others, the thought of ever respecting, appreciating, and loving yourself seems a long way off at the moment. I want you to know that I understand. I've been there, and so have many powerful and amazing women.

Please remember that you are not alone. If you have been very mean to yourself for a long time, then I know that this will take a lot of courage. But I believe in you. I know that you have that courage inside of you, just as I did. I'm not saying it's easy for everyone, but I am saying it's worth it. Despite the fact that I had been a big-time bully to the girl in the mirror for a long time, when I genuinely made amends to her, she became the most amzing friend I could ever have imagined. It was the best thing I have ever done. I used to think she was my enemy, but I could not have been more wrong.

Remember, I am with you every step of the way. When you

are ready, imagine that there is a girl you used to be friends with but with whom you've fallen out. Since then, you have been really mean and spiteful to her, making nasty, hurtful comments about her looks and constantly putting her down and making her feel that she is somehow not good enough.

After some soul-searching, you now want to make up with her and be friends again. What do you think you would need to say and do to get her to ever consider being friends with you again? What would you need to say and do to get her to ever feel that she could trust you again? I'm going to share with you what I did from A to Z, because it totally changed my life for the better.

This is a little heads-up that what you are about to do may make you feel vulnerable, possibly insecure, and maybe even scared. When those emotions come up, you'll want to shut them out. They'll feel uncomfortable, and so you may not want to feel them. Your mind will come up with excuses so that you don't have to face them, like, "I'm not doing this because it's weird to talk to yourself," or, "This is just stupid! You sound like an idiot!"[7] You may feel like skipping over this exercise completely because it's simply too hard to look at yourself in the mirror.

---

7   Well hello there, Little Miss Critical. We don't need your input right now, thanks!

I've been exactly where you are. For so long, it was far too painful for me to look at myself in the mirror, so I would either avoid it or, if I had to look at myself, I'd squint my eyes half-shut so that everything looked blurry and I couldn't see my "flaws." But, when I finally forced myself to look at the girl reflected back at me and really apologized for the pain I had caused her, I let go of a lot of that pain that I had been holding onto and took a massive step forward in building a strong and powerful relationship with myself. That's why I strongly recommend that you give this exercise a chance if you have ever hurt that girl in the mirror with anything you have said or done.

Think of it this way: If you said some really mean and nasty things to a little girl and then you realized that you had hurt her very badly, you would want to apologize, wouldn't you? If you hurt someone you love, you might even get down on bended knee to beg for forgiveness! And yet, we hurt ourselves every day with the negative judgments we make on ourselves. But we never apologize. This continues to build up, build up, and build up until it manifests itself in a really negative way. Right now is your opportunity to turn that all around and begin a positive and healthy dialogue with yourself.

Read, Look, Feel

1. Choose some time when you know you will not be disturbed, get your notebook where you wrote down all the nasty things that Little Miss Critical used to say to you, and go to a private place where you have access to a mirror.

2. Switch off your phone so that you will not be distracted.

3. Read the lists that you made of all the mean and hurtful things Little Miss Critical used to say and do to you. You can read them aloud or in silence.

4. Now, look at the girl in the mirror and notice how she's feeling.

5. Look into her eyes and see what's happening in them. Allow yourself to feel the depth of the pain, sadness, anger, or whatever other feelings you see there.

Apologize

When you are ready, tell the girl in the mirror how sorry you are for the things you have said and done to hurt her. Explain to her that you didn't realize that your words and actions were causing her so much pain, but now that you are aware of how awful your constant criticism and judgment made her feel, you want to do all that you can to make it up to her. You might say something like:

> "I'm so, so sorry for all the times I criticized you and made hurtful comments about you in front of other people and compared you negatively to others. You absolutely did not deserve that, and I am so, so sorry."

Add whatever you feel that you personally need to apologize for. Let it all spill out of you without judgment.

Forgive Yourself

Why do we need to forgive ourselves? Because guilt is a negative feeling, and any negative feelings that we are holding onto will interfere with the healthy flow of energy in our bodies and eventually end up stored as physical or emotional pain. By letting go of our negative feelings, we allow the energy in our bodies to flow freely. This makes us feel comfortable in our own skin, which makes us feel more confident and allows our light to shine.

However, we are all unique individuals, so some of us may feel guilt and others may not. Everyone has different experiences and different ways of responding to those experiences, so I want you to know that whatever you feel is totally okay. There is no right or wrong way to feel. But, whether you are aware of feeling guilt or not, you have nothing to lose by forgiving yourself anyway, because it might just make you feel a lot better.

So, how do you go about forgiving yourself? Well, the simplest way is just to close your eyes, put both hands over your heart, take a deep breath, and say:

"[Your name], I forgive you."

Take another deep breath and repeat:

"[Your name], I forgive you. I forgive myself for all the things I've done to hurt the precious girl inside of me. I didn't know what I was doing. I forgive myself and release any guilt I might be feeling about this."

Take another deep breath.

Repeat this process until you sense that any guilt you may have been feeling has completely gone from your body. How will you know if it's gone? You will know it's gone when you can breathe freely, easily, and deeply without any feeling of restriction. I'm talking about the kind of breathing where you can feel your ribs expanding to make room for the air going into your lungs and the oxygen tingling all through your body as it spreads—not little shallow breaths in your upper chest, but deep, healthy belly breaths!

Again, if you are feeling at all self-conscious about what you are doing, remember that nobody is watching you. You are doing this for you so that you can be happy and healthy and free. Who cares that you are talking to yourself? You've been talking to yourself inside your own head forever. We all do this!

Make a Gratitude List

Remind yourself of all the reasons you have to be grateful for your body. What has your body made it possible for you to do over the years? Think about it: if your body didn't function as well as it does, you wouldn't be able to do any of the things we take for granted that our bodies enable us to do every day.

Think back as far as you can remember and jot down in your notebook everything that your body has made it possible for you to do. It might be playing sports or a musical instrument, singing, painting, drawing, walking, skipping, reading, dancing, talking, cuddling, kissing? What are you personally grateful to your body for? Tell the girl in the mirror. Say:

"I'm so grateful to you for making it possible for me to..."

This is your way of saying, "Thank you for all that you've done for me and all that you do." Expressing gratitude will make you and your body feel happy. Psychologists from the University of California who researched the effects of gratitude in people's lives found that people who express gratitude daily are much happier than people who don't.[8] I have certainly found this to be true for me. Try it and see what it does for you!

Appreciate Your Reflection Daily

When we are young children, seeing our reflection in the mirror makes us smile and laugh and feel joy. Sometimes I babysit my friend's one-year-old baby girl, and she's an absolute delight to watch because she looks at herself in the mirror with nothing but positivity and happiness.

One day as I was watching her looking at herself in the mirror, I had a revelation. She didn't have one ounce of self-consciousness in her body; there was nothing but pure joy radiating out of her as she stood in front of the mirror rubbing her baby belly button and wearing nothing but her diaper. Her big blue eyes were full of joy at finding her belly button and tickling it. She giggled at her reflection and turned to look at me with excitement in her eyes. She was 100% in love with her body.

As I witnessed this unbounded joy, it actually brought tears to my eyes. It reminded me of when I was a little girl and how I used to kiss the mirror. Yep: I too used to find so much joy in my

8   Emmons, R. A., and McCullough, M. E., "Counting Blessings Versus Burdens: An Experimental Investigation of Gratitude and Subjective Well-Being in Daily Life." Journal of Personality and Social Psychology (2003), 84(2), 377–389.

reflection that I felt compelled to kiss it! Watching that beautiful baby reminded me that we are all born with 100% love for our bodies. But as we grow up, bit by bit, we get more and more self-conscious and less and less spontaneous. We start to compare ourselves negatively to others and find reasons to criticize rather than love the girl in the mirror. This isn't the pure and natural state that we were born into. We've been programmed to find flaws.

That gorgeous baby girl inspired me. I decided to take a leaf out of her book and try to find as much joy in my reflection as she did. What if, just like children, we all still found joy in our reflections? Wouldn't that be something? We'd be much happier and have lots more joy in our lives, that's for sure.

Of course, it requires a little effort and dedication on our part to counteract all of the negative programming we receive from society every single day—but it's totally doable! How about making it a part of your morning ritual to look in the mirror and, instead of focusing on the things that you don't like, *find at least three positive things that you appreciate about yourself that day.* Pretend that you are still that little girl who loved looking in the mirror and never thought of looking for "flaws." It's time to take back the happy energy of the little girl who only found happiness and joy in her reflection.

This is one of the things that I did that really helped me to go from hating my body to loving it. I started to look in the mirror every morning and to find at least three positive things to say to myself about my reflection. This certainly wasn't easy for me in the beginning. It was a huge challenge. I had to push through the resistance and force myself to find three things that I could admire. However, it became easier over time, and it even began to feel natural to smile at my reflection rather than cry. If this is too difficult for you to do in the beginning, then just look into your own eyes in the mirror. Don't look anywhere else. Just look into the eyes of the girl in the mirror and tell her that you love her. From there, you will eventually be able to appreciate other parts of yourself.

I am convinced that learning to love and appreciate my body with all its "imperfections" has played a major part in my achieving the body confidence that I am so grateful to feel today. The transformation within me really hit me not so long ago in the fitting rooms at H&M . Fitting rooms were something that I used to do my best to avoid because I couldn't face looking at myself in a big, three-way mirror with that harsh department-store lighting. But since I've been learning to love my own reflection, this process has become so much easier.

So there I was in this tiny cubicle, whipping off my dress to try on a new pair of jeans. The old part of me wanted to squint my eyes so I wouldn't have to see my reflection clearly, but the new loving and compassionate part of me told me to be brave, open my eyes, and look in the mirror. And what happened? I cried. I had tears streaming down my face within moments. Except this time, these weren't tears of pain. These were tears of absolute joy.

As I opened my eyes, only positive and loving thoughts showered over me, and I felt like I had finally learned to love and accept the girl reflected back at me. It was a huge win for me. It was actually magical. It affirmed to me that all the work I had put in, all the pain I'd pushed through, and all the hurdles I'd overcome had totally been worth it. I felt so free, and for the first time, I felt confident standing there in that fitting room.

What had changed? My mindset had changed. I'd successfully reprogrammed my mind to only think loving and positive thoughts when looking at my reflection, and in return, even what I saw reflected back at me had transformed. I desperately want this for you, too. You deserve to feel the joy that comes from loving the girl in your mirror. And you can!

In the beginning, it might be hard to focus on loving parts of your body that you have been feeling a lot of negativity towards. For example, I would have found it very difficult to begin with my thighs, just because they were a part of my body I'd always felt negativity towards. But that's okay. I got there eventually, and so will you!

You can begin by appreciating parts of your body that you may have forgotten about, or just taken for granted. Here are some easy examples to start with that you can say to yourself whenever you look at your reflection.

"Hey, you know what? You've got beautiful hands! I love your fingers and gorgeous nails."

"And you know something else? I love the way your nose crinkles and your eyes light up when you giggle!"

"Girl, you've got lovely ankles (or hands, or arms, or teeth, or eyes, or neck, or cheekbones, or eyebrows)."

Gradually, you will get more and more comfortable with appreciating things about yourself. Eventually, you will be ready to move on to accepting and appreciating the parts of your body that you used to criticize the most. Be gentle and patient with yourself while doing this. Notice what emotions come up for you.

Do you feel sad? Angry? Embarrassed? Does it feel painful? If so, where do you feel that sadness, anger, embarrassment, or pain in your body? Hold your hands over that painful area and gently rub it as you breathe deeply. One of my painful areas was my tummy. This was such a sensitive place for me because it was where I stored a lot of negative thoughts about myself. To acknowledge and remedy this, I would rub my tummy gently and tell it that I loved it. I would say, "I love my tummy. Thank you for looking after me." It might seem silly, but it really, really helps.

So, if you're feeling emotional about a particular area of your body, that's okay. Be gentle with yourself. Please try not to run away from what you are feeling or to do something else to take your mind off of it. The emotion you are feeling is just your body telling you that the energy is stuck in that area and it is now ready for you to release it. I know that this may seem scary in the beginning. Little Miss Critical will be itching to pop in and give her opinion, but you know how to deal with her now, right? Just give her a silly voice and float her out of your headspace, and then allow Kindness, Positivity, and Gratitude to help you to appreciate, accept, and love all parts of you, including the parts that you used to dislike the most.

After some time and practice, you will get more and more comfortable with appreciating yourself and it will become completely natural to look in the mirror and smile at the girl looking back at you. When I do it these days, it always makes me feel uplifted and gives me an instant confidence boost. This practice takes less than a minute, but it can fill you with a positive feeling for the rest of the day! Remember that:

What you think and feel is simply reflected back at you.

What you see in the mirror is a reflection. If your body is filled with negative emotions such as hate and disgust, that's what will be reflected back at you. If you can look in the mirror and smile, a smile will be reflected back at you. If you can learn to appreciate and praise your body and see it for the unique beauty that it is, what will you see when you look in the mirror? A beautiful, happy girl!

Be Proud To Be You!

You may not be aware of this yet, but there's a power and a beauty inside of you that is so much greater than your external appearance. Soon, you will feel ready to connect with and celebrate that inner beauty and strength and become the powerful, self-confident young woman you were meant to be. Whenever you need a pick-me-up or you're about to do something that scares you—or even just before you go to school in the morning—here is a quick and easy way to harness your inner Supergirl confidence.

1. Stand tall in front of a full-length mirror with your feet shoulder-width apart, your shoulders back, your head and eyes facing forward, and your hands placed powerfully on your hips.

2. Breathe deeply into your belly; you will instantly feel a boost of kickass Supergirl confidence! Exhale.

3. Hold this powerful pose for a moment, breathing naturally, and then look into the eyes of the girl in the mirror and say aloud:

"Today, I love and accept all parts of myself."

Take a deep breath in and exhale slowly.

"I am good enough, and I don't need to prove it to anyone. I am proud to be me."

Take another deep breath in and exhale slowly.

"I am capable of anything I put my mind to."

Take another deep breath in and exhale slowly.

This is a great way to reprogram your body and your brain for happiness and success. Your body posture affects not only how you feel about yourself, but also how other people treat you. Simply by changing the way you hold your body, you can instantly boost your confidence and lift your mood. Plus, saying these positive statements whilst holding this Supergirl pose wires the truth of them into the networks of your brain. With repetition, your brain will accept what you are telling it. So go on, step into your Supergirl power and let your light shine brightly! Look in the mirror and tell yourself:

"I am beautiful! I am awesome! I am powerful!"

Because it's true.

Make a Commitment to Yourself

Are you totally ready now to let go of the old, negative way you used to think and feel about yourself and embrace a happy, healthy, and fulfilling future with your new best friend? Of course you are! To show your commitment to your friendship with the girl in the mirror, I would like to suggest something that I didn't think of doing for myself, but wish that I had. (You will find out why in a later chapter).

Let's take a pledge together that reminds us of the loving and compassionate way we now promise to treat ourselves. I've framed my pledge, and it hangs on my bedroom wall so that I see it every morning when I wake up. Write yours down and place it somewhere you will see it every day.

I, [your name], commit to loving myself today exactly as I am.

I promise to do my best to think only positive, loving thoughts about my body and to change my thoughts immediately if I forget.

I promise to do my best to avoid negative self-talk when I am alone and with others and to apologize to myself immediately if I forget.

I promise to look in the mirror every morning and every night and say at least three positive things to the beautiful girl looking back at me.

I promise to listen to what my body is telling me it needs and to care for it in the way I would care for the person I love the most in the world.

Find a special, visible place to keep your personal commitments so that you will see them every morning when you wake up. You are leaving an old disempowering habit of criticizing yourself in the past and creating a new empowering habit for yourself. And the best way to train your brain into accepting this new habit is through constant repetition and reinforcement.

Even with the best of intentions, it's very easy to forget about our commitments. I certainly did, and I'll explain how in a later chapter. For now, make life easier for yourself by putting yours in a place you will see it and be reminded every morning. You might like to pin it on the inside of your wardrobe/closet door or even above your mirror. If it's not something you want others to see in your bedroom, how about placing a heart above your mirror that represents all the love you're going to give yourself? That way, nobody else needs to know what it means to you, but every time you see that heart it will be a signal to you to smile at your reflection in the mirror.

Big Sis Memo

Please don't give up on yourself after a few days. Remember that learning to love the girl in the mirror is a journey, and you're only just starting out. The further along the road you go the easier and more enjoyable it will become.

As you focus on loving the girl in the mirror, you'll notice how you start to feel positivity and love in other areas of your life, too. When you feel lovable, you experience a world that loves you back! What you give to yourself is what you will attract in return from those around you. When you love and accept yourself for who you are, you radiate an energy of self-confidence that other people find very attractive.

I encourage you to look in the mirror and see your best friend looking back at you. She's with you every single day, through the highs and the lows. She loves you. Love and accept her for who she is. Become best friends with the girl in the mirror and your life will be so much happier than you ever thought possible.

Chapter Summary

In this chapter, you've:

- ♥ Become aware that the most important relationship you will ever have is the one you have with yourself.

- ♥ Come to understand the importance of making amends to the girl in the mirror for the way you treated her in the past, if that is relevant for you.

Making amends means:

- ♥ Owning up and taking responsibility for your past behavior

- ♥ Apologizing

- ♥ Forgiving yourself

Three additional steps to becoming best friends with the girl in the mirror are:

- ♥ Make a Gratitude List

- ♥ Appreciate three things about your reflection daily

- ♥ Make a commitment to accept, love, and appreciate yourself from now on

You've also discovered how to step into your Supergirl powers and be proud to be you! You go, girl!

How much time have I wasted on diets and what I look like? Use your time and your talent to figure out what you have to contribute to this world. And get over what the hell your butt looks like in those jeans!
—America Ferrera

CHAPTER 5

Ditch the Diet and Eat to Be Happy and Healthy!

After reading this chapter, you will:

- ♥ **Never want to go on a diet again!**

- ♥ **Have discovered some shocking truths about what is actually in many of the foods and drinks that are advertised as "healthy."**

- ♥ **Never be fooled again by misleading food marketing.**

- ♥ **Know what it is that your body really needs to thrive and be happy.**

- ♥ **Have the knowledge you need to make food your friend and to enjoy it without worry or guilt.**

How do you feel about food? Do you love it and feel great eating it? Do you love it and feel bad after eating it? Or does food totally frighten the heebie-jeebies out of you so you don't know what to think or feel? Back in my days of hating my body, I thought food was my enemy. Either I was scared of the calories in everything I ate because I thought it would make me put on weight, or I would stuff my face just to feel some sense of being full—then I'd feel guilty about it afterwards and make myself throw up. There was very little happy balance for me when it came to food.

I would go from one diet to another, constantly looking for the next "miracle" that would help me lose weight. At the beginning of each new diet I would feel optimistic, but after a few days I would begin to feel hungry, deprived, and miserable. Back then, I believed that the only way to be healthy and stay slim was to:

😔 eat as little as possible

😔 eat as low-fat as possible

😔 not feed my body when it was hungry.

I was so wrong!

Surprise, surprise—I never really lost much weight from dieting. In fact, over time, I put more weight on. This made me so angry with myself! I'd be a crying mess on the bathroom floor every time I stepped on the scales. The more weight I put on, the more I hated myself and the more destructive I became with food. I would either starve myself or stuff myself.

But now, thankfully, that has all changed for me. Not only do I **never diet,** but I have also fallen in love with food again. I eat when I'm hungry, I never deprive myself, and I don't even own a scale! Oh, and guess what? Even though I eat more than I did before, I'm the happiest and healthiest I've ever been.

"Hold on a minute," I hear you say. "How did all that happen?"

Well, on my journey to loving the girl in the mirror, I've

discovered some amazing things about the relationship between our bodies and the fuel we put into them. I'm not a dietitian, doctor, or fitness guru, but from my own experience and from the tons of research I did during my healing journey, I have learned a lot about how our bodies respond, both physically and emotionally, to what we feed them.

This new knowledge has totally revolutionized my relationship with food, and it's had such a crazy-good impact on my body—so much so that I now want to shout it from the mountaintops so that every girl and woman in the world knows about it.

I. Am. So. Excited. To. Share. This. With. You.

Can you tell?

Bye-Bye Dieting

How does the word "diet" sound to you? Just the word alone for me conjures up feelings of emptiness, hunger, and lack. It makes me think I'll be depriving my body of something it desperately wants and needs. Ugh. However, in today's society, we've been programmed to think that this is the way to lose weight, remain slim and/or "be healthy." But that's totally mixed up. The shocking truth is that dieting can actually make us gain weight! Yes, you read that right.

Doctors at the University of New Mexico have found that when we starve ourselves and deprive our bodies of essential nutrition, we cause an upset in our hormonal system that actually causes us to hold onto weight.[9] This is supported by recent

9   https://www.unm.edu/~lkravitz/Article%20folder/metabolismcontroversy. html

research at the American Dietetic Association, which found that teenagers who diet are three times more likely to be overweight five years on than teenagers who don't diet.[10]

Does this shock you? To be honest, if someone had told me this a few years ago I would have been shocked, but by the time I discovered the science behind it all, I already knew from my own experience that this was true. The scientific explanation completely backed up what my own experiences had been— it just felt like the pieces of a jigsaw puzzle were finally coming together to reveal the bigger picture about my relationship with food.

What Happens to Our Bodies When We Diet?

When we diet or have a very low-calorie intake over a period of time, our bodies go into something called "starvation mode." This is a wonderful survival mechanism that nature very kindly gave to our prehistoric ancestors to keep them alive during times when there was a shortage of food. What has that got to do with us today in the twenty-first century where food is available 24/7 for most of us?

Well, quite a lot, really! You see, the part of our brain that is responsible for our survival hasn't caught up with our lifestyle in the modern world. Our primitive brain doesn't understand that we would choose to deprive ourselves of food and nutrition just because we want to lose weight. In other words, it doesn't understand the concept of "dieting." As far as our brain is concerned, if our body is not getting the calories and nutrients it needs to function properly over a period of time, then that must

10 http://www.weightlossresources.co.uk/eating_disorders/teenage-dieting.htm

mean that there is a shortage of food and we are in danger of starving to death. So, in a desperate attempt to keep us alive for as long as possible, our brain does two things:

1. It sends a message to our body telling it to slow its fat-burning rate way down in the hope that our existing fat stores will last until more food becomes available.

2. At the same time, it releases the hunger hormone (ghrelin) to motivate us to eat—or, in the case of our prehistoric ancestors, to go out and hunt or forage for food!

Isn't it amazing what our bodies do to keep us alive? Just think: if our ancestors hadn't had this survival mechanism, we might never have been born! We've got to admit that Nature knew what she was doing when it came to our ancestors, but where does that leave us today if we want to lose weight? It's certainly not great news if you're thinking of doing it by dieting, as I, and millions of others, have found out.

When we diet or otherwise deprive ourselves of the nutrition we need, after a while our body stops burning fat. And, as you will know if you've ever done this, you also get very, very hungry! That's because of the hunger hormone telling you that you need to eat. Now, if you listen to your body at this point and you eat a healthy meal that gives your body the nutrients it needs to function properly, all will be well—just like when our ancestors found food in our distant past.

Your body might not start burning fat straight away—not until it is sure that there's going to be more nutritious food tomorrow. But, if you continue to eat normally and your brain is convinced that there is enough food available, then your body will begin to use up its fat stores for energy and balance will be restored.

But what if you don't listen to what your body is telling you it needs at this stage? What if your desire to lose weight is so strong that you try to fight your hunger? Many of us are able to do this for a while, but it seriously messes with our moods and our metabolism and is totally counter-productive in the long run. In some people it can even lead to anorexia, which is a very serious condition.

Big Sis Memo

To any girl reading this who is—or even suspects she might be—suffering from anorexia, please, please confide in a trusted adult and ask for help. Everything in this book can help you, but if you are losing or have lost a lot of weight very quickly, you know that you are not eating enough, you are lacking in energy, have unstable moods, or any combination of the above symptoms, please see a doctor or ring one of the organizations listed at the back of this book in the Resources section.

Help is available. You are not alone in this.

There are wonderful people out there who can help you, and they are just waiting for your call. I really want you to know that you are important and you are loved. Please love yourself and that precious girl in the mirror and ask for help to get well. I promise you that you will be so glad you did.

For most of us, when we have been dieting for a while, our natural survival instinct eventually kicks in. Our brain will keep bombarding our body with an SOS in the form of the hunger hormone until eventually we can't stand it any longer and we give in. And, in my experience, when we have reached this level of uncontrollable hunger, we don't usually eat a healthy, nutritious meal unless one happens to be right in front of us at that very moment. And how likely is that? Yeah, not very. We're more likely to grab some junk food that has lots of calories but little to no nutritional value—we'll also probably eat a lot more of it than we normally would because we feel so hungry and deprived.

What happens next? Because our body hasn't been getting enough nutritious food for a few days (or weeks!) leading up to this binge, our primitive brain thinks that there is a shortage of food. So it sends a message to the parts of the body that control metabolism, saying, "Slow right down. Don't burn those calories. We need to build up our fat stores!" The result of this process is that we gain weight that we probably wouldn't have gained if we hadn't been dieting. And to top it all off, our body *still* hasn't got the nutrition it needs, so it's still hungry.

For many of us, this is just the beginning of the downward spiral that leads to Misery Street, because now we've put on weight and we feel terrible about ourselves, so we go on another diet to try to lose the weight we've gained, and guess what happens? Yeah, exactly the same thing all over again. If we keep on going from one diet to the next, we put on a bit more weight each time, which is exactly what happened to me when I gained about 25 pounds over 3 years!

My "Aha!" Moment

Back in my dieting days, I didn't know any of this. I was depriving myself of one of my greatest pleasures for nothing. Because of this, not only did I put on weight, but I also felt sad, miserable, and, eventually, hopeless. I missed food soooo much, and I don't know about you, but when I'm sad and miserable, I certainly don't feel healthy or attractive. I don't feel excited about life and I don't feel like being active. With every diet I went on, I was telling my poor body again and again that it wasn't good enough. I was trying to force it to fit into a "perfect mold" by starving it, and it just wasn't working. Instead it was damaging and counterproductive.

The final straw, as well as the big epiphany, came for me when I was 19. Feeling desperate and confused about why I couldn't lose weight and thinking that I might have a hormonal imbalance that was causing the problem, I went to see a doctor. That's when something began to shift in me—but it wasn't the weight.

The doctor put me on a diet of 1,000 calories a day that had virtually *no* fats in it. It was fat-free everything! She told me to eat only the "foods" on her diet sheet for one month and then return to her with my results. I did exactly what she told me to do, and that was one of the most miserable months of my life. I frequently cried myself to sleep and I had no energy. At the end of the month, I had lost a very small amount of weight, but nothing that was worth how miserable and lacking in energy I was feeling.

It was because of how awful I felt, both physically and emotionally, during that month that I made the decision to give up trying to lose weight and accept myself exactly as I was. The thought of putting myself through the misery of another month like that was just unbearable.

I am really grateful for that experience now, because it put me off dieting for the rest of my life and also turned out to be the beginning of a whole new happier and healthier life for me. It's funny how things that seem terrible at the time can turn out to be for the best in the long run.

So, What Did I Do?

I started to eat again. I wanted to be happy, and I knew that I could never be happy if I continued to deprive myself of something I loved so much: food! I am a "foodie." I love food and I've loved cooking ever since I was a little girl, but that had all stopped when I started dieting. I wanted to get that joy back into my life. I wanted to enjoy food again and be able to eat with my family and friends without feeling guilty.

I have to be honest and say that, because I was already suffering from an eating disorder at this stage, the transition didn't happen overnight for me. There were still parts of me that were scared of food for a while, but that fear gradually got less and less severe, especially when I saw what a positive impact eating right was having on my body.

You see, when I stopped the stupid fad dieting and decided to love myself exactly as I was, my instincts and habits started to change. Instead of reaching for the junk food to fill my emptiness, I started to enjoy finding out how to *nourish* my body with food. I wanted to take care of my body, so I tried to listen to what it was telling me it wanted.

The more I accepted and appreciated my body just as it was, the more it began to crave the good stuff. For the most part it wanted healthy, home-cooked meals, and I let it have what it wanted. As I got stronger and more loving towards myself,

I started to relax more and more around food. If I sometimes fancied pizza or a piece of chocolate, I would have some and I would tell myself to enjoy every bite. The desire to binge went away almost immediately when I started to allow myself to enjoy eating.

I began to feel a lot better both physically and emotionally. My mood improved dramatically, the tightness in my body relaxed, and the constipation (Overshare, I know! But I warned you that this was my brutally honest story.) that I had been suffering from for years disappeared. I had stopped attempting to fit into a "perfect mold," and it felt pretty darn liberating.

I was getting happier, and the happier and more relaxed I became, the more the excess weight I had been holding onto melted away without me even trying. People close to me even started to notice how happy and healthy I looked. It felt so amazing to be eating normal amounts of food again and I began to feel excited, even passionate, about experimenting with different ingredients and creating new, delicious recipes to share with family and friends. My energy levels rose dramatically and, at the risk of sounding weird, I not only fell back in love with food, but I also began to fall back in love with life, just like the little girl I used to be who loved to kiss the mirror.

What brought about this miraculous change? How could I lose weight while eating as much as I wanted when I'd hardly lost any when I was restricting my diet to only 1,000 calories a day? Again, I am not medically trained, but based on my research into nutrition and how our bodies work and from my personal experience, I believe that it is due to a combination of a few things:

1. I was now being kind to my body and treating it with love and respect, so it was more relaxed, less stressed, and happier, which means that it was no longer constantly over-producing the stress hormone (cortisol) that plays havoc with our metabolism.[11]

2. My brain knew that there was plenty of food available from eating regular meals, and because of this it was now free to tell my body that it was safe to burn fat.

3. My body was getting all the nutrition it needed to give me energy and to stabilize my moods, so I no longer had the same cravings for the kind of "food" that has loads of empty calories.

Eat to Thrive, Not Just Survive!

On my healing journey, I discovered that the food I eat has a massive effect on how I feel. Some food makes me feel energized, awake, healthy, and glowing, and some can make me feel moody, irritable, slow, and sleepy. If I were a car, I'd say that back in my dieting days I used to fill my tank up with cheap, low-grade fuel that kept my engine turning over, but only at a fraction of my potential. When I stopped dieting, however, and began to treat my body like a slick sports car that deserved the best-quality fuel, the difference it made was literally life changing. It was the difference between surviving and thriving.

Over the last couple of years, I've been nourishing my body so that it thrives. I eat delicious, yummy foods, I have loads of energy, and I don't have to worry about putting on weight. I honestly don't. I haven't weighed myself in over two years. I

---

11 See Chapter 6 on stress for more about this topic.

simply go by how I think and feel. And, with the knowledge I'm going to share with you, I hope that you will discover which foods you can eat to make your body thrive too.

First, let's take a look at the different kinds of fuel available so you can choose which one you would prefer to put into your body.

The Low-Grade Fuel

Highly Processed Foods and Drinks

What do I mean by "highly processed?" Obviously, all the food we eat is processed in some way. As soon as a piece of fruit is picked from a tree, it has been "processed" simply because it's no longer attached to the tree. However, it is the extent to which something is processed before it passes your lips that determines if it's low or premium-grade fuel for your body.

It's simple, really. The less that's done to it to change it, the better it usually is for you, and the more that's done to it to change it into something else, the lower the grade of fuel it is for your body. Think of the difference between a piece of fruit or a vegetable and a packet of chips (crisps in the U.K.) or a donut. The apple and the vegetable are still an apple and a vegetable when we buy and eat them. They are still in their natural state. The chips and the donut, on the other hand, started out as potatoes and wheat, but they go through many different mechanical and chemical processes before they reach our tummies.

The potato, for example, ends up in a factory where it is peeled, sliced, mixed with salt, sugar, a bunch of artificial flavors and preservatives, fried in hydrogenated oil, and put into a packet. As for the donut, well, you don't need me to tell you about that. Have you ever seen a field of donuts? This is not to say that you can't enjoy a bag of chips or a donut for a treat every once in a while. I certainly do! But it's something to keep in mind when your first impulse is to go for these sorts of foods.

Highly processed foods like these have plenty of calories but little or no nutritional value and, to make matters worse, the combinations of potentially harmful additives and preservatives in them are often specifically designed to make us overeat and to keep coming back for more.

You can often recognize highly processed foods by looking at their labels. Anything that has a long list of ingredients that you've never heard of before is likely highly processed, and also likely contains loads of stuff that has very little business being in the human food chain. Your body deserves so much more than this low-grade fuel.

Sugar: the Sneaky Food Bandit

Sugar is in most highly processed "foods" and drinks, and is often disguised behind a different name such as sucrose, dextrose, barley malt, maltose, sucralose, rice syrup, or HFCS (High Fructose Corn Syrup). Research carried out at the National Centre For Biotechnology Information showed that sugar alters our brain chemistry in the same way that drugs do, leading to binging, cravings, and withdrawal symptoms. In fact, in 2015, Dr. James DiNicolantonio published a review that explained that in an animal study, "even when you get rats hooked on an IV of cocaine, once you introduce sugar, almost all of them switch to the sugar."[12]

---

12 http://www.independent.co.uk/news/science/sugar-has-similar-effect-on-brain-as-cocaine-a6980336.html

Now, that is pretty darn scary to me. What do you think?

The more sugar we consume, the more we crave it. It controls our energy levels and creates mood swings. On top of that, a recent Yale study[13] found that eating or drinking sugary stuff increases our appetite. This is because sugar interferes with the signals between the body's hormones and the brain, so the brain doesn't receive the message that the body is full. So, when we eat or drink a lot of sugary stuff, we tend to consume more than we would normally because our brain still thinks we're starving. Our brain then also slows down our metabolism so that we don't use up our fat stores too quickly.

The tricky thing is, sugar is not just in the places we would expect it to be, like in fizzy drinks and junk food. It's also hiding in places where you might least expect it. For example, there are lots of products on the supermarket shelves that are labeled "Low Fat", "Fat-Free", and "Zero Fat". This is a great advertising trick because it misleads people into thinking that, if they eat or drink this product, it will help them lose weight because it's low in fat. Nope!

You see, when fat is taken out of products such as yogurt, it doesn't taste so great anymore. So what do the manufacturers do to make it taste better? They add sugar. The result is that, although these products do contain less fat, most of them are packed full of sugar. This won't help you to lose weight at all, because sugar actually converts to fat in the body. So when I'm grocery shopping, I don't go for the low-fat option or focus on the calories. I look at how much sugar the product contains and I'll go for the option that has the least added sugar.

---

13 http://www.laweekly.com/restaurants/certain-sugars-stimulate-appetite-study-finds-2894554

Try this out: Have a look at the labels on food, particularly in low-fat or sugary foods, and you'll see the sugar content somewhere in grams. 4g of sugar is the same amount as one teaspoon of sugar. So a yogurt that has 24g of sugar in it is like adding 6 *teaspoons* of sugar to your snack! In fact, here's a little exercise for you. Go and pick an item of food in your cupboard or fridge and read the label to see how much sugar is in it. Then, get a glass and a teaspoon, and for every 4g of sugar in the food product, pour a teaspoon of sugar into the glass. When you've finished, you can clearly see just how much hidden sugar is in that product.

What's A Girl to Do?

This all might sound quite scary, but it doesn't have to be! When I began to do research and discover what's actually in the food that I eat, it made me feel excited about finding the best foods to nourish my body and keep it in tip top condition. This meant that I no longer had to despair over putting on weight, so I stopped feeling the need to harm my body by forcing it to throw up. It led me down a path of happiness and health that I am so grateful to be on every day.

Believe me, I still eat yummy and delicious things; it's just that I now pick the option that has been processed the least and has the least amount of sugar in it. When I'm cooking, I sweeten my food with minimally processed ingredients like fruit, honey, maple syrup, dates, raisins, and coconut. I have really enjoyed discovering great new ways of making delicious, healthy desserts and cakes without using sugar.

So, if you have a sweet tooth, don't worry. Cutting out sugar does *not* mean that you have to give up on sweet things. It is easy to make delicious, healthy, nutrient-rich desserts and cakes using real raw ingredients instead of refined sugar and chemicals—and they taste so much better than the synthetic stuff, too!

I feel so passionate about this because of the huge difference just a few simple changes in what I eat have made to the way I feel about myself. So, if you only make one conscious decision to make a positive difference in how you nourish your body today, let it be that you become aware of the sugar in your food. This doesn't mean obsessing. This doesn't mean not eating. This doesn't even mean reducing the amount food in your daily diet. It means considering alternative versions that may contain less sugar and, as a result, it means taking an incredible bad-ass leap forward in feeling like you're in the driver's seat of your own life, moving towards loving and feeling great in the skin you're in.

Now that you know what's in the low-grade fuel you've been putting into your body, let's take a look at the premium fuel that will enable your body to function at its best.

The High-Quality Fuel

"Natural" is a tricky word. Sometimes food companies use the word "natural" on their packaging to make us think that their product is healthy and not highly processed, but a lot of products with "natural" on their labels are just as full of refined sugars and oils, preservatives, and dubious additives as other products.

When I talk about "natural" foods, I'm talking about the foods that are as fresh and as close to their natural state as possible. These are full of the essential nutrients our bodies need to feel happy, healthy, and full of energy. Here's a simple checklist of the things most bodies need on a daily basis:

Good Fats

Yes, fats! Your body actually needs yummy, good fats in order to thrive. That's why I felt so miserable on the fat-free diet that the doctor had put me on, and also why I didn't lose much weight. That was a huge wake-up call for me. I now realize how massively important good fats are for stabilizing our moods; preventing us from feeling tired, irritable, anxious, and depressed; reducing our cravings for sugary foods; boosting our metabolism; and giving us energy. I now eat plenty of them throughout the day because I know they give me brainpower, make my skin glow, and help me to maintain my happy, healthy weight.

Here are some easy ways to get good fats into your diet every day:

♥ Avocado: Add to smoothies, spread on toast or sandwiches, make it into guacamole, or simply add a side of avocado to any meal.

♥ Olives

♥ Extra Virgin Olive Oil: Drizzle on top of vegetables or use as a salad dressing.

♥ Nuts: Almonds, Brazil nuts, macadamia nuts, walnuts, hazelnuts, pecans, and pine nuts are all just a few of my favorite nuts to snack on. Just a couple of any of these keeps me feeling full and energized for hours. Much better than a bag of chips! I also love organic nut butters; in fact, one of my favorite snacks is an apple dipped in almond butter. So yummy and healthy!

- ♥ Seeds: chia seeds, flax seeds, hemp seeds, pumpkin seeds, sesame seeds, sunflower seeds

Nuts and seeds are not only easy sources of good fats, but they are also excellent sources of protein, fiber, minerals, and other important nutrients that we girls need to keep us healthy and glowing. The mineral zinc, for example, is essential for healthy skin and really helps if you suffer from acne or PMS.

Fresh Fruit and Vegetables

You can't really eat too much fresh, organic, yummy fruit and vegetables. They are packed full of vitamins and minerals that our bodies need to stay healthy and they are full of fiber that makes our digestive system very happy. Bye-bye, constipation! (Again, oops, overshare. #sorrynotsorry!) If you can't get organic fruits and veggies, then pick the next-best option and wash or peel them before eating, just in case any unnecessary additives or pesticides have been sprayed on the outside.

Now I know that some people don't love vegetables like I do, but if that's you, then I'll bet it's because you made your mind up when you were a child that you don't like them and you've not really given them a chance since then. Now that your taste buds have matured, you might view vegetables in a completely different light—especially if you learn how to prepare them in delicious ways. There are so many tasty ways to enjoy vegetables, both cooked and raw, and I don't want you to miss out, so here are a few of my favorite ways for you to try:

- ♥ If you have a juicer, you can make delicious nutrient-packed drinks with any fruit or vegetable you fancy and you can adjust the taste to your own liking using lemon/

lime/ginger/ice/coconut-water/mint and loads of other yummy ingredients that cater to your own taste buds. If you've never had one, you have a real treat in store. I'd better warn you that they are addictive (in a good way!), but your body will love you for it. I have at least one a day and they make my cells zing with energy. Visit www.girlunfiltered.com/recipes for mouth-watering recipe ideas.

♥ A yummy smoothie: If you prefer a creamier, dessert-like treat, then try a naturally colorful smoothie made from a couple of handfuls of any fruits of your choice, like blueberries or strawberries, some leafy greens like kale or spinach, a spoonful of almond butter or half an avocado for your good fats, and top it all off with a cup of almond milk. Turn on your blender or smoothie-maker and presto, there you have a delicious snack packed full of goodness! Trust me, it won't taste like you're drinking spinach. You can even add some nuts or seeds to give it a bit of a crunch if you like, or a little honey if you want more sweetness. The sky's the limit once you start getting creative, and it's soooo easy that anyone can do it! If you Google "healthy smoothies," you'll get a host of fun recipes you can experiment with.

♥ Salad: Add color and crunch to your meals with a side salad of raw vegetables. It only takes a couple of minutes to throw one together. I use some leafy greens and top them with things like cucumber, peppers, olives, and celery, but you can make your salads with any kind of vegetable you like. It's good to use different colors of vegetables as this not only makes your salad look prettier but also gives you a wider variety of nutrients. Make your own salad dressing with olive oil and balsamic vinegar or lemon juice!

♥ Roasted vegetables: This is my favorite way of doing vegetables, and it's so simple. Just pour a tablespoon of olive oil or coconut oil onto a baking tray and sprinkle some sea salt (or any seasonings you like!) over it. Next, roll your broccoli, carrots, sweet potato, kale, or any vegetable you fancy in it. Pop the tray in the oven and bake at around 400°F/200°C for 15 to 20 minutes (some veggies need different temperatures and cook times, but this is a good starting point for most vegetables, except kale, which only takes five minutes). You won't believe how delicious vegetables can taste.

♥ Veggie snacks: If I'm feeling hungry in between meals, I sometimes snack on veggies and fruit. I love to dip cucumber, celery, or carrots in hummus! Bananas dipped in almond butter are also so yummy and a great snack before I go on a hike or take a dance class.

Protein

Our bodies simply couldn't survive without protein. We need it to maintain our muscles, bones, blood, and internal organs. Protein also keeps our metabolism working! But we don't only get protein from meats, as many people think. In fact, sometimes I go for weeks being a vegetarian and I still eat lots of protein. Here are just some of the proteins I eat at least once a day, and they can be cooked in so many yummy ways which makes every meal time different.

- ♥ Fish and seafood

- ♥ Lean, grass-fed meats /poultry

- ♥ Tofu

- ♥ Lentils

- ♥ Beans

- ♥ Eggs

- ♥ Grains like quinoa or soba noodles

- ♥ Nuts and seeds

Carbohydrates

We need carbohydrates to give us energy, and cutting them out of our diet is not a good idea—trust me, I tried it. I felt lousy, headachy, and had zero energy. However, some carbohydrates are better at sustaining our energy than others. Picking the right ones can make a ton of difference to how our body feels.

Some carbs like white bread and certain pastries are made from refined white flour that has had most of the nutrients and fiber removed, so they aren't as beneficial for the body as those that are made from the whole grains. I'm not saying you should never eat them, but you just don't want your main source of carbohydrates to come from these kinds of foods. I eat pasta, rice, and bread, but I choose the wholegrain versions that I know will make me feel better. I even make my yummy homemade pancakes on Sunday mornings as a treat, but instead of white flour, I use coconut flour and add bananas and blueberries for sweetness. So delicious!

Here are a few healthy ways of getting good carbohydrates in your diet:

- ♥ Use brown rice instead of white rice when you can.

- ♥ Pick bread that is made from mostly whole wheat, rye, or spelt flour that has minimal or no sugar added to it. If you ever feel bloated or uncomfortable after eating bread, try a gluten-free bread for a little while and see if that makes a difference.

- ♥ The grain quinoa is a complex carb that contains both protein and carbohydrates. A double win! It is so easy to cook and is really delicious. Try cooking it with some vegetable stock instead of water for added flavor!

- ♥ Try whole wheat, spelt, or brown rice pasta as an alternative to regular pasta.

- ♥ I love potatoes: boiled, mashed, or in their jackets. However, they leave me feeling sleepy, so I only ever have them in the evening now. Try and see how they are for you.

- ♥ Sweet potato is great for me at any time. I love it baked, mashed, or grilled. Sweet potato fries baked in the oven are a yummy but healthy comfort food.

- ♥ Eat leafy greens! Yes, even green veggies contain good carbohydrates!

♥ Oatmeal is a fantastic way to start the day off by boosting you with energy and fiber. When I say oatmeal, I don't mean the powdery stuff that comes in packets and has sugar and artificial flavorings added to it—you can get organic rolled oats in most supermarkets. Make it into oatmeal/porridge or use it to make a delicious muesli with nuts, raisins, and seeds. It's *so* delicious and it has no added processed sugars but will keep you feeling energized for hours.

Water

Okay, I know water isn't technically a food group, but it is so, so vital to our health. Even if you only made the decision to drink more water throughout the day, I'm sure you'd already feel more energized. The more water I drink, the healthier my skin is, the clearer I can think, and the less I crave sugary foods. I can't even remember the last time I had a sugary, fizzy drink or can of soda—I feel much better after a glass of refreshing water. Try to drink about eight big glasses (about two liters) a day.

If drinking eight whole glasses of tap water sounds too boring to bear, some fun ways to get the water you need is by mixing up the daily eight with plain sparkling water, unsweetened herbal tea, and/or making your own fun "spa" water with cucumbers, lemons, limes, mint, and even fresh ginger in it!

Make Food Your Friend

Now I put premium fuel in my body whenever I can, and I look and feel so much better for it. I enjoy preparing and cooking my own meals because then I know I'm packing them full of vitamins, minerals, and good fats, which all help to keep me happy, healthy, and in tip-top condition. I *never let myself go hungry*; I always carry healthy snacks with me throughout the day. You'll always find a banana, apple, or bag of nuts or seeds in my handbag.

Although most of my diet now comes from natural and fresh produce, I'm not obsessive about it, and I certainly don't want to make you start worrying about every single thing that you eat. I still enjoy going out for pizza or sharing a dessert with girlfriends on a night out. As long as I'm aware of what I'm putting into my body and I feel happy eating it, then I believe my body is happy to process it. I've made food my friend; I no longer fear it or feel out of control around it. I respect it, I appreciate it, and I'm grateful for it.

I know that at certain times when I crave excess comfort food or my desire to binge comes back, it is usually because of something emotional going on within me that I haven't yet processed. Once I realize this, I make time to tune in to how I am feeling, give myself some attention, and do some tapping (see Chapter 7), and the craving goes away.

I also believe in being really loving and gentle with myself when I'm feeling vulnerable, just as I would be with an upset child or with my best friend, so I will give my body a treat if it wants one and really allow myself to enjoy it. If I decide to eat some chocolate, I do it consciously. I'll savor the flavor and texture of it. I'll enjoy every single bite. In this way, I can really enjoy and appreciate the chocolate and, after one or two squares, I feel satisfied. I feel like I have been loving to myself.

The way I eat now is so different from the unconscious way I used to eat when I would just wolf down food without really tasting it or chewing it. Now, when I prepare a meal, even when it's just for myself, I try to arrange the food on my plate so that it looks pretty. I add color with some green vegetables and then maybe some carrots, tomatoes, or red and yellow peppers for contrast. It doesn't take much to make a meal look special, but it's worth the effort because of the way it makes you feel. It's a way of saying "'you're special, and you deserve the best!"

You don't have to drastically change your diet all of a sudden or become super hung up on what you eat in order to start making healthier choices. It's not about obsessing; it's about loving yourself. A really empowering question you could ask yourself is: "How could I really love and nourish my body with food today?" It could just be a matter of making a few adjustments to your meals. Simply cutting down on the sugar in your diet and adding a few things, such as good fats, to your daily food routine could make a huge difference to how you feel. Or, it could just mean thinking up some yummy alternatives to the snacks you usually eat, such as substituting raw nuts and seeds for salty and sugary snacks and cutting out sugary and diet drinks and drinking more water instead.

I know that, while you still live at home, you pretty much have to eat the food your family eats, but this could be a fun journey for the whole family to go on together. Even though I don't even live on the same continent as my family anymore, they have all become really interested in eating healthily now, too. My mum, dad, and even my younger brother now make their own juices and smoothies, and my mum and I often message each other recipes and photos of the lovely food we create. It can be a great way to do some family bonding.

These are just some ideas of how you can make food your friend, but most importantly, *appreciate* the food you eat. Learn to listen to your body and start asking yourself, "Do I feel good eating this?" If the answer is yes, then enjoy every bite! If it's no, then look at the reasons why and enjoy finding some alternatives that might leave you feeling more "yes." Remember, there's a big difference between eating something because you hate yourself and eating something because you love yourself. Appreciate every bite from a place of love.

Visit my website www.girlunfiltered.com for some great ideas on how you can easily add more essential nutrients to your daily diet, plus some really easy but delicious recipes—even if you've never cooked before!

Chapter Summary

In this chapter, you've learned that:

- ♥ Teenagers who diet are three times more likely to be overweight in the future than teenagers who don't diet.

- ♥ When you diet or significantly reduce your calorie intake below what your body needs to provide energy and essential nutrition, your body goes into "starvation mode" and stops burning fat.

- ♥ Highly processed foods tend to be "low-grade fuel" for your body. They are full of calories but have little or no nutritional value, so your body is still starving for nutrients even though you may have eaten a lot.

- ♥ Refined sugar can be as addictive as certain drugs! The more you eat it, the more you crave it, and it wreaks havoc with your body and your emotions.

- ♥ It is really important to get enough "good fats" in our daily diet. They make us feel full for longer, give us energy, speed up our metabolism, regulate our hormones and our moods, make our skin glow, and on top of all that, they taste awesome!

As much as we've talked about overeating (and the impulse to consume foods that don't nourish us very well) in this chapter, we haven't dug that deeply into one of the major things that makes us do just that—stress. But don't worry; we're headed there next.

What *is* stress, anyway, and why does it cause us so much trouble? Let's find out together.

You can't rely on how you look to sustain you. What actually sustains us, what is fundamentally beautiful, is compassion...compassion for yourself and for those around you. That kind of beauty inflames the heart and enchants the soul.

—Lupita Nyong'o

CHAPTER 6:

Five Simple Stress-Busters for Your Busy Teenage Life

In this chapter, we're going to talk about the stress that comes with being a teenage girl in today's world. You will discover:

♥ what exactly stress is

♥ where it comes from

♥ how it can affect your body in ways you really don't want, and

♥ my top five stress-busters for keeping the Stress Gremlin at a manageable distance!

Nobody should ever underestimate the pressures that a girl has to deal with during her teenage years: the schoolwork, the deadlines, the exams, the many social pressures and hurdles, the expectations (your own and other people's) of fitting in, family, friends, relationships, keeping fit, college applications, maybe even a part-time job—it makes me stressed just thinking about it! It can easily get overwhelming. Stress levels can go through the roof if you're feeling pressures from too many sources at once, and if this stress is not managed well, it can have a negative effect on your physical, emotional, and mental health.

I believe that it was those pressures—together with my unrealistic desire to be perfect—that were the major causes of me developing an eating disorder. There were so many "uncontrollables" in my life. I needed to have some control, so I tried to control my body. At that time, it was the only way I knew how to cope with the stress I was experiencing. I never confided in anyone about the pressure I was feeling, so I felt very alone with it. Looking back, I wish I had talked to someone. I wish I had opened up to my parents. I even wish I had talked to some of my teachers. I now know that they could have eased that anxiety and worry. Please, don't be afraid to admit you're finding it hard to cope if this is something that's bothering you. You're not the only one!

The thing is, when you're in that situation, you don't even feel like you have time to think about how you could make things easier for yourself. You're constantly running like a caged mouse on a wheel, just trying to keep up with everything. For me, it felt like I was always focused on the future and what I needed to do to achieve whatever goals I had my sights set on; not only in my school exams, but pretty much in everything I did. I rarely took a time-out to just be in the moment, to chill out and relax, and even when I did, I would always end up thinking about what needed to be done later that day, tomorrow, next week ...

I know I was not alone in feeling that way. All teenage girls may not be perfectionists, but most of them still feel pretty stressed out by all the demands placed on them. Unfortunately, there's not a lot we can do to change those outside demands. The education system is as it is, and if you're planning on going to college, then you have to study hard to get the required grades to get in. Furthermore, it's often not enough just to get the required grades, is it? For many universities, you also need to be able to:

- ♥ Provide evidence that you are a responsible, enthusiastic all-rounder who plays music and/or sports at a high level.

- ♥ Show great organizational and leadership skills, as well as evidence that you're a team player who cares deeply about the environment and does charity work in her spare time!

Whoa, sister, that's *a lot* of pressure. And I am not joking about any of that, as you will know if you have reached the stage where you are doing university applications.

I'm not suggesting for one moment that you opt out of this system if you want to go to college and earn a degree. There is a lot to be said for developing some of the above skills and qualities, and I am really grateful to my school for giving me the opportunities to do that. However, there are better ways to cope with the pressures associated with these challenges than I was aware of at the time. So, let's take a look at what stress really is, where it comes from, how it affects us, and how we can ease it.

What Is Stress, and Where Does It Come From?

"Stress" is a word we now use in the modern world for something that even our caveman ancestors experienced—except they usually felt it for different reasons. In order to survive long enough to reproduce and become our ancestors in the first place, they had to be able to put up a good fight when stalking their prey or sprint away quickly to escape when they were in danger. But nature was kind enough to give them an inbuilt automatic response to help them to survive. This response is called the **"fight or flight"** response because it gives the body the ability to fight harder or run faster when under threat. Thankfully, we still have that same automatic response today when we are in danger.

I was very grateful for it one day when I was out walking my dogs in the fields near my home. I was completely engrossed in playing fetch with my two dogs, so I didn't notice that the gate between the field I was in and the next one was open. Suddenly, the ground began to shake. I turned around and saw a huge herd of cattle barreling into my field at top speed and coming right at me! A rush of adrenaline pumped through my body and, in a split second, my dogs and I were sprinting to the nearest place of safety. I only just managed to throw myself over a fence a few seconds before I might have been trampled to death by about forty sets of thundering hooves!

You can imagine how hard my heart was beating when I landed on the safe side of the fence. When my dogs came running up to me to check that I was okay, I realized that I was panting harder than they were. My muscles were tensed like iron fists as I hunched over, hands resting on my knees, trying to catch my breath while the cattle jostled with each other for the best position to stick their heads through the gate and watch me.

Gradually, as the realization that I was safe sank in, my breathing and heart rate slowed down, my muscles began to release the tension of the sprint, and I started to cry with relief as the shock and fear started to leave my body. Within a relatively short period of time, my body had relaxed and returned to normal functioning and I felt grateful for my narrow escape. The stress response had saved my life! There had been a genuine threat to my safety, and my body had done what it needed to do to survive.

So, what was that, exactly?

Well, as soon as I heard the thunder of hooves, a few things happened automatically in my body without any conscious thought on my part whatsoever:

- ♥ A bunch of hormones, including adrenaline and cortisol, flooded into my system.

- ♥ My breathing quickened to allow an increased flow of oxygen to my muscles.

- ♥ My arm, neck, shoulder, and leg muscles tensed up to prepare my body for fight or flight.

- ♥ My heart rate went into overdrive and my blood pressure skyrocketed to make sure more fuel reached the parts of my body where it was needed (arms, legs, and brain).

- ♥ My mouth went dry as my body stopped producing saliva to avoid adding digestive enzymes to my stomach.

- ♥ My body stopped digesting my food so that the blood could be diverted to my arms and legs.

- ♥ Perspiration seeped out of my pores to keep my body cool.

And then—*and this is really important*—when the danger was over and I knew I was safe, my body went into recovery mode. My breathing slowed down and became deeper again. My heart rate returned to normal and my muscles relaxed. This is how nature intended the fight-or-flight response to work. It is only supposed to last for a few minutes—the time it would normally take to either escape, or be killed. If you've survived the danger, your body is supposed to go into recovery mode immediately. This is so all the systems in the body that had to stop functioning temporarily while you were escaping can return to normal.

When you were reading my story about being chased by a herd of stampeding cattle, did you notice any change in your own breathing? Maybe it sped up or maybe you noticed that you were holding your breath? Were you aware of your muscles tensing up or your heart beating faster than usual?

As we've already touched on in previous chapters, our minds and our bodies are very connected, so...

What we think about or imagine has a huge effect on the way we feel.

Very few of us face life-threatening stress triggers (such as stampeding cattle) on a regular basis, but it is good to know that our fight-or-flight response is there to help us if the need arises. However, what we *don't* want is for that stress response to keep kicking in at times when we don't need it—which is most of the time.

Here's the problem. The part of our brain where the stress response comes from is a primitive part of our brain; it has not evolved to keep up with our lifestyle in the modern world. It's still somewhere back in caveman times when our ancestors really did have to deal with frequent threats from predators such as wild animals. Unfortunately for us, our primitive brain can't tell the difference between a real threat to our survival and an imagined threat. This means that every time we have a fearful thought like "I'm never going to be able to cope with all the work I have to do," or "I'm going to fail my exam," or even "I have nothing to wear to the party," that primitive part of our brain thinks our life is in danger. And what does it do? It automatically activates the fight-or-flight response. There's no herd of stampeding animals or any dangerous predator to fight or to run away from. So where does that leave us?

With a big load of STRESS! STRESS! STRESS!

And that stress doesn't just go away all by itself. It stays in our body like a pain in the neck (literally) until we do something to change the chemistry in our body and stop the stress response. If we really had to fight or run for our lives, we would release the stress chemicals and muscle tension in our bodies, and then, after the threat was over, our bodies could relax and return to normal functioning. But, because the things that stress us today are more likely to be our own negative thoughts, or a fallout with our friends, or a school assignment that we're finding difficult, our bodies get all worked up and have nowhere to let all that energy out on a regular basis.

All those stress chemicals and hormones are going around and around in our system, wreaking havoc on everything from our metabolism to our emotions. The result is that we can end up with a whole load of stress-induced symptoms such as: feeling anxious, nervous, tense, irritable, tired, numb, tearful, having negative thoughts, headaches, upset stomach, acne, weight gain, problems sleeping... the list goes on!

When Little Miss Critical used to shout in my ear telling me that I wasn't good enough, it caused me to feel almost constant stress. This caused my body to overproduce hormones that actually prevented me from losing weight no matter how hard I tried. My body was so tense and blocked that normal functioning shut down. I would never have lost any weight or felt any healthier if I hadn't first gotten rid of Little Miss Critical, changed my ways of thinking, and learned to manage my stress.

I am so thankful to be way more in tune with my body now, so I can instantly tell if something doesn't feel right within me. If I feel bloated or constipated, I know that I'm holding onto something that's worrying me emotionally. If I find my chest is constricted and my breathing is shallow, I realize I'm not managing my stress levels effectively and my anxiety is flaring up. That's when alarm bells ring and I know that I need to make more time for the stress-busters that work for me, so that it doesn't spiral out of control.

One of the most loving things any of us can do for ourselves and for those in our lives is to learn to control our stress response rather than let it control us. There are several really effective stress-busters that will help you feel way more in control of your stress levels. Here are my favorites!

My Top Five Stress-Busters

Stress-Buster One: Exercise

Everybody knows that exercise is good for you, but it's also one of the best stress-busters there is. I always feel like I've cleared my mind and released tension from my body after running, dancing, or hiking out in nature. Physical activity releases endorphins (happy hormones) that can lift our mood and make us feel much better.

I know that not everybody is wild about exercising, and what you don't want is for your stress-buster to become an additional stress. The trick is to find a form of exercise that you will enjoy. Make it fun! Yoga, running, dancing, hiking, skipping, swimming, and biking are just some fun ways to manage your stress levels.

For people who are used to playing sports, the idea of an hour of exercise five times a week is no big deal. They look forward to leaving the pressures of life behind and just being in the zone for a while. However, I know this is not the same for everybody, at least not to begin with.

If you can only fit in 15 minutes some days, that's fine. Make the most of the time you've got and enjoy it. If you're really struggling to fit exercise into your day during particularly busy times, then do 30 jumping jacks or dance wildly in your bedroom (check out Chapter 9 ... you'll see!) every few hours. It will only take you a minute or two, but you will still feel the benefit if you really focus on being happy and "in your body" during that time.

Here's a little tip to get the most out of this stress-buster: Whatever form of exercise you are doing, smile while you're doing it! Smiling lifts your mood. It sends a signal to your brain to release your feel-good hormones—serotonin, dopamine, and endorphins. Smiling relaxes your body. Go on, try it for yourself. It's pretty hard to feel stressed when you have a big smile on your face.

Stress-Buster Two: Breathe Like a Baby!

Have you ever noticed how your breathing changes when you're feeling anxious or scared? Remember the stampeding cows? (Yeah, me too!) When we're stressed, our breathing quickens to send more oxygen to our muscles to prepare them to fight or to run away. Without thinking about it, we start taking fast, shallow breaths in our upper chest. This is exactly what we need to do if we're getting ready to fight or run away from danger, but it is the exact opposite of what we need to do when we want to remain calm and focused in our normal daily lives.

If we are constantly getting ourselves all stressed up about stuff, however, we get into the habit of breathing this way all the time. Then, because we're breathing this way, our brain picks up the signal that we're under threat, so it pumps more stress hormones into our body and we keep going around and around and around on an unhelpful stress Ferris wheel.

The good news is that we can neutralize the stress response simply by changing the way we breathe. Yeah, it really is that simple! If instead of taking rapid, shallow breaths in our upper chest—which causes us to get all pumped up—we start breathing slowly from our belly, like a baby does, that will cause us to relax and stop the whole stress cycle. If you watch a baby breathing, you will see that their belly expands when they inhale and deflates when they exhale. This is why they're called "belly breaths." There is very little movement in their chest and shoulders. The air simply flows deep down into the lungs and expands the belly, and then flows back out again.

Try this out for yourself for one minute:

1. Sit up straight with your back supported by a chair or lie down on your back with your knees in the air and the soles of your feet flat on the floor (or the bed).

2. Place your hands on your tummy, just below your ribcage, on top of your belly button. Close your eyes and focus your attention on where your hands are placed.

3. Take a slow, deep breath in so that your belly expands.

4. Exhale slowly through your mouth as you silently count "1...2...3...4...5," and notice how your belly deflates like a balloon with the air going out of it.

Keep breathing slowly like this for a few minutes while focusing on how your ribs swing out as your belly expands each time you breathe in, and on how your belly deflates like the air going out of a balloon when you exhale. If your mind starts to wander away from this exercise to think about other things, gently bring it back to focus on the feeling of your breath moving in and out of your lungs and the count to five on your exhale.

Breathing like this for a few minutes will reduce stress and anxiety. It also takes your awareness away from the worries in your head and quiets your mind. I recommend that you practice breathing like this several times a day so that it becomes second nature to you. It will keep your stress levels down and help you to neutralize the stress response if you feel it coming on (and you are not in any real danger).

When you practice this consistently over time, your body will begin to breathe more fully and deeply without you even having to think about it. This will help keep you feeling relaxed and calm. By the way, you don't need to put your hands on your tummy to breathe like this. That was just to remind you to let your belly expand when you inhale and deflate when you exhale. You can breathe like this any place at any time, and nobody will notice!

Any time you feel stress coming on, you notice that your breathing is speeding up, or you're holding your breath, just gently focus your breath down into your tummy and slow your breathing right down. This will help you to relax, calm down, and become more focused. This is a super-great practice for exam nerves and performance anxiety of any kind!

Stress-Buster Three: Get Enough High-Quality Zzzzz's!

The quality of the sleep we get plays a huge role in how we feel the next day. I'm sure you know what I'm talking about. We've all experienced lack of proper sleep at some time or another, and how does it make us feel? Miserable, irritable, lacking in energy, jumpy, hungry, unable to concentrate, close to tears, and even depressed. Basically, when we don't get good sleep and enough of it, our natural defenses are down and we are stressed out physically, mentally, and emotionally.

You see, a whole bunch of things happen in our bodies while we're asleep to keep us functioning properly. If we don't get enough good quality sleep, the hormonal balance in our bodies gets upset, and so does our brain's capacity to solve problems and remember things we've learned. I know there can be a lot of pressure on us at times that makes it difficult to get a good night's sleep, such as too much homework; worry about relationships with parents, friends, and boyfriends or girlfriends;

a test we need to cram for, and any number of other things that cause us worry and stress.

Believe me, I've been there. It becomes an ever-increasing downward stress spiral that affects every aspect of our lives. It even affects our appetite, because the hormones responsible for making us feel hungry (ghrelin) and full (leptin) can become imbalanced through lack of sleep. When we're sleep-deprived, ghrelin levels go up, which makes us feel hungrier, and leptin levels go down, which means that we don't feel full even though we've eaten more than we need.

Okay, now that we know how important sleep is in combatting stress, what can we do to make sure we get enough of it? The best way I've found is to create our own personal bedtime routine. As you already know, our brain responds to signals, so we want to create a relaxation routine that sends a signal to our brain that we are getting ready to sleep.

Try this out:

> Set a regular bedtime and stick to it. If you've not been doing that up until now, it may take a little while for your brain to get the message that this is now your time to sleep, so it may take a few days for your body clock to adjust.

> Stop all activities that are not part of preparing for sleep at least a half-hour before you get into bed. This gives your brain a signal to shift from daytime activity mode to sleep mode.

> Shut down all social media and switch your phone off!

This is so important. The bright light on mobile phones, tablets, and laptops confuses our brains and makes us think that it is still daytime.[14]

Dim the lights in your bedroom. This gives a signal to your brain to produce melatonin, the hormone that helps you fall asleep and stay asleep.

Choose some gentle, relaxing things to do to help you wind down. Have a warm, relaxing bath with lavender oil; light a nice-smelling candle; listen to some relaxing music; read a book (not a textbook, and not on your phone or device) or magazine; do some gentle stretching to ease the tension out of your body.

Clear your mind. If you have a lot of "mind chatter" going on in your head about things you have to do the next day or things that are worrying you, keep a notebook or journal by your bed and write them all down. In this way, you are getting them out of your head and essentially storing them someplace else for the time-being so you can sleep. Also, if you find that you have good ideas for a project or essay popping into your mind while you're trying to sleep, just jot them down in the same notebook so you know you can remember them in the morning.

---

14 https://www.scientificamerican.com/article/q-a-why-is-blue-light-before-bedtime-bad-for-sleep/.

Big Sis Memo

Do you remember how I said (at the beginning of this chapter) that the things that cause us stress in the modern world are usually our own thoughts? Those thoughts are usually either about things that happened in the past or things that we imagine will happen in the future. We spend most of our time in a different time-zone than the one we're actually in—and that would be okay if it was productive for us in any way or if it made us feel happy. But does it? Well, to be fair, sometimes it does make us feel happy to daydream about future happy events. I love to indulge in that kind of happy fantasizing sometimes. Who doesn't?

But what if it's not making us feel happy? What if, instead of imagining pleasurable and exciting things that might or might not happen in the future, we are worrying and "catastrophizing" about things that might never happen? This is not only stopping us from being productive in the here and now, but it is also creating a huge amount of unnecessary stress and anxiety in our lives that prevents us from enjoying the present.

The next two stress-busters really help me to know that I can cope with whatever the future brings and also to remain calm and productive in the present moment.

Stress Buster Four: Look at the Worst-Case Scenario

Instead of blowing things out of proportion and worrying about "catastrophes" that might happen in the imagined future, take a step back and ask yourself this: "Okay, what's the worst possible outcome in this scenario?" You might be causing yourself a lot of unnecessary stress and anxiety by letting your mind get carried away with "what ifs," like:

What if I don't get good enough grades?

What if the boy or girl I like doesn't like me?

What if I don't make enough money at my summer job to pay for that trip I've been wanting to go on with my friends?

What if I fail my exams?

What if? What if? What if?

When you stop and ask yourself "what's the worst that can happen?" you'll usually find that, if you answer this question honestly, it won't ever be as bad as you were worrying about. It really won't be the end of the world if any of the above things happen. There are always options, and there are always ways to work through things if you can just take a step back, breathe, and ask for help when you need it and when the situation calls for it.

I used to put so much unhealthy pressure on myself to get perfect grades at school. This would make me so stressed out that my chest would feel tight and my stomach would feel nauseous because I placed so much expectation and fear onto it. One day, I decided to ask myself "Literally, Helena, what is the worst thing that could happen if you don't get the grades you want?" And guess what? It wasn't nearly as catastrophic as I'd feared. The absolute worst-case scenario would have been that I'd have had to repeat my exams. Although that wouldn't have made me feel ecstatically happy, it certainly wouldn't have been the end of the world, either. When you allow yourself to look at the worst-case scenario and know that you can cope with that, if it happens (which it hardly ever does), it takes the mega fear out of the "what if?"

Even though I no longer have to worry about school grades, I still use this simple question when I find myself getting all stressed up and worried about something that hasn't happened and might not ever happen. It helps me when I have to go through unsettling changes in my life by accepting the challenge head-on rather than fearing it. It helped me when I moved 6,000 miles away from my family, it helps me when I'm about to go on a big audition, and it even empowers me in my relationships. By asking myself such a simple question and being honest with myself when I answer, I'm able to gain a much better perspective on the situations in my life. I realize now that how I feel about myself and my life is not dependent on anything or anyone outside of myself; it depends on how I choose to interpret things...and that's such an empowering feeling!

Stress-Buster Five: Be Mindful of the Present Moment

Sometimes my to-do list is so long, I want to hyperventilate when I look at it. It's at times like these I have to tell myself to stop running around like a headless chicken thinking about the million and one things I have to do and instead ...

just...

...stop.

I give myself a moment to take a deep breath and focus on where I am and what I'm doing in the here and now. If you really think about it, it is counterproductive to worry about things that might never happen in the future, because while you're doing that, you are causing yourself unnecessary stress and you are not being as effective as you could be in the present! Of course, this is different from planning ahead—we're talking about worrying ahead, here. Similarly, it is a total waste of your time and energy to be stuck worrying about something that happened in the past, because, well, it's in the past and there's nothing you can do to change it. That's why becoming mindful of the present moment is an amazing stress-buster. That means completely focusing on what you're doing as you're doing it.

One of my favorite times to do this is when I'm eating. If I have a beautiful, yummy meal before me or a delicious snack to enjoy, then I want to be completely mindful of the present moment as I eat. This practice not only helped me to fall back in love with food, but it also helped me to get more in-tune with my body, which certainly helped my healing process!

This little trick works for everything; especially when stressful feelings or emotions are starting to take over. Simply:

Stop.

Breathe.

Focus on how you feel in the present moment. Not how you felt ten minutes ago and not how you might feel later. Just right now. Focus on how your body feels. You can even focus on what your surroundings are like. How does it feel to sit on that chair, or stand on that floor? Is the air surrounding you warm or cool? Is there a breeze? What can you hear? Smell? Taste? Be fully present in the here and now instead of letting your mind wander to the future or the past.

This is actually a great way to work your way through your to-do list or to complete homework. By mindfully focusing on the task at hand, rather than letting your mind wander off to either the past or the future, you'll be able to manage your time a lot more efficiently and effectively.

Chapter Summary

In this chapter, you have learned that:

- ♥ The "fight-or-flight" response is nature's way of protecting us.

- ♥ The "primal" part of our brain can't tell the difference between a real and an imagined threat to our survival.

- ♥ The way we think about ourselves and our lives can cause us massive stress, and it doesn't have to be that way.

- ♥ The stress response is only supposed to last for a few minutes and then the body should naturally go into recovery mode.

- ♥ When your body is trapped in stress mode, you can help it get back to a healthy balanced state by using the five stress busters outlined in this chapter.

How are you feeling, gorgeous girlie? Look at how far you've come. You might already be beginning to notice your inner confidence increasing as you discover all the ways you can take charge of your own feelings and your own life. It's so empowering. But, if that isn't happening yet, don't worry. This is a journey, and you have a right to travel at whatever speed you're comfortable with. You are unique and wonderful exactly as you are, and perseverance is much more important than speed.

Shall we see where we're going next? Let's go!

Let me be myself and then I am satisfied. I know that I'm a woman, a woman with inward strength and plenty of courage.

—Anne Frank

CHAPTER 7

Tap Your Way to Health, Happiness, Freedom, and Success

In this chapter, you'll learn:

♥ A simple yet effective technique that will empower you to take charge of your own thoughts, feelings, and actions and tap into your own highest potential (literally!)

To watch a demonstration of this incredible technique, head to www.girlunfiltered.com/tapping where I have video tutorials waiting just for you!

The incredibly powerful tool that I am about to share with you has helped me enormously on my journey from loathing myself to loving myself. This magic tool is called "tapping," and it made it possible for me to heal myself of bulimia—plus much more!

One night after I had decided I wanted to stop being bulimic, the urge to make myself sick was so strong that I could feel my skin crawling. My body began to itch and I started pacing up and down the room. I was determined to overcome the need to purge, but how could I do this when my mind was screaming at me to throw up? I began to cry and get really upset. I was torn between two voices in my head: one telling me that I'd better throw up quickly, and the other telling me that this was completely wrong and that I wanted to stop this terrible habit. Luckily, I broke down in tears with my mother, admitted to her that I was bulimic, and told her how scared I was.

That night, my mother, who is a psychologist, taught me how to tap. She told me she had been using this magic tool with her clients for years and she knew it would help me. She was right. I couldn't believe how much better I felt after just a few minutes of doing this silly little thing!

To begin with, tapping does seem like a really silly thing to do. If I hadn't been so desperate for help that night and if I hadn't known for sure that my mother would never joke with me at such a time, I would have thought she was pulling my leg! I'm so glad she wasn't.

So, what is tapping?

Just what it sounds like! It involves tapping with the tips of your fingers on certain points on your body while focusing on whatever you're feeling at that time. It works like magic by reducing the intensity of the feeling in just a few minutes. Yes, in just a few minutes, the uncomfortable feeling can almost disappear. Your body calms down and returns to a more balanced and peaceful state.

In earlier chapters, we saw how thinking negative thoughts leads to negative and/or uncomfortable feelings in your body. That feeling can then make you want to act in ways that can be destructive to your physical or emotional wellbeing, such as eating a load of junk food, experimenting with unhealthy substances, or harming yourself in some other way. It's like a chain reaction that begins with a thought, leads to a feeling, and ends with an action or behavior that is not loving towards yourself.

Take a look at this visualization of a negative chain reaction:

Negative Thought

Uncomfortable Feeling

Unloving Action

Tapping interrupts this chain reaction at the root of the feeling so that you have no need to carry out the unwanted behavior. For example, if you tell yourself "I'm fat" or "I'm not good enough," or "My body is ugly," this can cause you to feel depressed, dejected, hopeless, etc. When you feel these things, it can cause you to act in ways that will harm your body and/or make the original "problem" worse. In my case, this was starving myself until I got so hungry that I would binge and then purge. But rather than just deciding not to think the negative thought anymore and hoping you'll feel better, tapping goes way deeper by healing the energy disturbance that the negative thought has created in your body.

When I was bulimic, my negative chain reaction went like this. It usually began with Little Miss Critical saying something like:

1. You're not good enough. Your thighs are too fat.

2. I feel inadequate; I feel unattractive.

3. I hate my body.

4. I starve myself.

5. I feel hungry and miserable.

6. I eat much more "food" (i.e. empty calories, etc.) than my body needs.

7. I feel disgusted with myself.

8. I make myself throw up.

Tapping enabled me to interrupt the negative chain reaction at point #2 so that I no longer needed to act in a way that was harmful to my body.

Let me show you how that's possible.

Look again at the graphic above showing my negative chain reaction. Do you see how it all began at point #1 with the negative thought "my thighs are too fat" and quickly went to point #2 where I feel inadequate and unattractive? Okay, so here's how tapping works:

I notice that I'm not feeling great inside—that I'm feeling upset about something. Maybe I've just tried on a new pair of jeans and I don't think I look great in them, or I've just seen another girl looking stunning and I compare myself negatively to her.

I check inside of myself to see what's really going on. I ask myself "What am I thinking?" and "What am I feeling?" I get that I'm thinking that my thighs are too fat and that I'm feeling "not good enough."

I ask myself to rate the intensity of the feeling on a scale from 0 to 10, where 0 means that it's not bothering me at all and 10 means that I'm feeling so upset and disgusted with myself that I really hate my body. I feel that it's about a 4 at the moment. It's still quite low on the scale because I'm only at point #2 on the chain reaction and I've caught this feeling very quickly. I also know that if I don't do something to stop the chain reaction now, the feeling will get more and more intense.

I begin to tap gently on the pressure points of my body (shown in the diagram on the next page) while saying the phrase: "Even though I'm feeling 'not good enough' and I think that my thighs are too fat, I still love and accept myself completely."

After I've done three rounds of tapping while focusing my attention on feeling "fat and not good enough," I take a deep breath and check inside to see how I'm feeling now. Because I've caught the negative feeling before it has had time to snowball into something worse, it is very likely that it will have gone down to a 1 or a 0 on the intensity scale after just these first three rounds of tapping. However, tapping still works even if you've already gotten much further down the chain reaction, although it might take a little longer.

For example, the night my mother taught me how to tap, I was already at a 10 on the intensity scale before I started. The feeling of wanting to purge was so intense that I felt like jumping out of my skin—and yet, after just a few minutes of tapping, it went away! I felt calmer and stronger and I no longer felt the need to throw up. It was like a miracle. I was so proud of myself knowing that I had managed to overcome the overwhelming desire to purge that had been controlling me for so long. After that, I used tapping any time the desire to binge or purge resurfaced and, no matter how intensely uncomfortable my feelings were in that moment, I would find myself feeling calmer and stronger and sometimes even smiling after just a few rounds of tapping.

How Do You Tap?

The trick is to tap lightly with your fingertips on certain pressure points on your body (see diagram on facing page) whilst repeating a few words that describe how you are feeling at that moment in time.

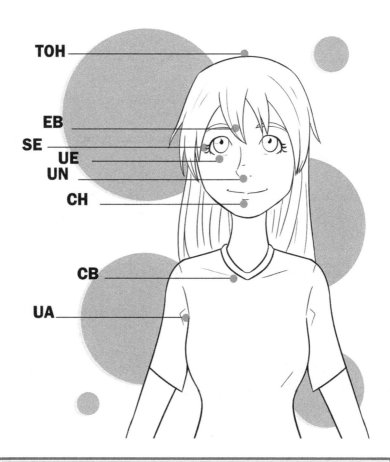

TOH: Top of the head

EB: Eyebrow (just where your eyebrow begins)

SE: Side of the eye

UE: Under the eye

UN: Under the nose

CH: The indent between the mouth and the chin

CB: Collarbone

UA: Under the arm (where the band of your bra is)

Step One

Ask yourself, "How am I feeling right now?"

When you identify your feeling, it will likely be something like:

"I feel sad/lonely/stressed/angry/depressed/anxious/fearful/ overwhelmed."

Now, rate the strength of your feeling on a scale from 0–10, where 0 means you don't feel it at all and 10 means it is as intense as it could be.

Now, place whatever you are feeling within the following sentence:

"Even though I feel [feeling], I still love and accept myself completely."

If you find it too difficult to say that you love and accept yourself to begin with, you could say "I am choosing to love and accept myself" instead.

Here are some examples:

"Even though I hate my body, I am choosing to love and accept myself completely."

"Even though I feel disgusting, I am choosing to love and accept myself completely."

"Even though I feel sad, I still love and accept myself completely."

This is called your Setup Statement.

Now, repeat your Setup Statement aloud three times as you tap the "karate chop" point on one of your hands with the fingertips of your other hand. (The karate chop is on the outside of your hand, midway between where your hand joins your wrist and the base of your little finger.)

Step Two

Once you've said your Setup Statement three times while tapping your karate chop point, it is now time to tap on each of the pressure points labeled in the diagram. Use your fingertips to tap gently from one pressure point to the next, starting with the top of your head. Tap about seven times on each point following the order below:

1. Top of your head

2. Eyebrow

3. Side of your eye

4. Under eye

5. Under nose

6. Under your lips/beginning of chin

7. Collarbone

8. Under the arm where the band of your bra is

As you tap on these points, say a "Reminder Phrase" out loud to help you to focus on the feeling. For example, if you were feeling angry, you might say:

"I'm angry" or "all this anger."

You may notice that you begin to yawn as you keep tapping. That's great. It means the stuck energy is shifting!

Complete three cycles of tapping, beginning and ending with the pressure point at the top of your head, while saying your Reminder Phrase aloud.

Step Three

When you've completed three rounds of tapping, take a deep breath in and exhale slowly. How strong is the feeling now on a scale from 0–10? If the number has gotten smaller, that's great. Sometimes the negative feeling is completely gone after the first three rounds of tapping, and other times it takes a little more tapping before you feel relief. Just keep tapping until the feeling no longer bothers you and it's either at zero or a very low number on the scale.

Well done!

You've just taken control of your thoughts and changed your feelings from negative and uncomfortable to calm and balanced. Can you see how being able to change your thoughts and feelings in this easy way gives you freedom and power and opens up wonderful possibilities for your life?

Tapping is a fantastic healing tool. It makes it possible for you to reverse all the negative junk in your head that is acting as a barrier between what you would like to see in the mirror and how your thoughts and feelings are causing your body to behave. I was never able to achieve a happy and healthy body when I was stuck in a negative mindset. It was only when I came back to a loving and balanced place within myself that the anxiety, self-hatred, and excess fat I was holding onto began to melt away. I am so grateful to tapping for helping to get me there so quickly and so easily.

Other Ways To Use Tapping

Tapping can be used to process any emotion that is making you feel uncomfortable. It is brilliant for managing cravings, stress, anxiety, fear, and all uncomfortable emotions that cause you to feel out of balance and prevent you from feeling free, happy, confident, and energized.

Here are some other examples of Setup Statements that might be relevant for you from time to time:

"Even though I'm feeling stressed and under a lot of pressure, I'm now choosing to be calm and focused."

"Even though I judge my body, I am willing to love and accept myself."

"Even though I am not perfect, I am willing to love and accept myself."

"Even though I feel lonely because it seems like nobody understands what I'm going through, I still love and accept myself completely."

"Even though I'm nervous about my exam, I choose to feel calm, confident, and focused."

"Even though I feel excluded at school, I still love and accept myself completely."

"Even though I feel like throwing up, I still love and accept myself completely."

"Even though I'm frustrated at myself, I am still choosing to love and accept myself completely."

"Even though I'm feeling really upset right now, I still love and accept myself completely."

"Even though I'm experiencing this craving for ice cream, I still love and accept myself completely."

"Even though I feel like a failure, I choose to love and accept myself completely."

Another name for tapping is Emotional Freedom Therapy (EFT), and when you try it for yourself, you will understand why. This simple yet powerful technique can set you free from being a victim of your own negative thoughts, feelings, and habits and clear the way for you to become the happiest, healthiest, and most successful version of yourself.

Happy Tapping!

Chapter Summary

In this chapter, you've learned that:

You have the power at your fingertips to completely reprogram your thoughts and feelings in a very short period of time.

The easiest way to learn to use this powerful technique for yourself is by heading to the EFT section on my website, www. girlunfiltered.com. Let's tap together!

Instead of judging your fears, invite them to tea. Offer them a cookie and have a chat. Listen to what they have to say.

—Kris Carr

CHAPTER 8

Listen to Your Fears, But Don't Let Them Drive the Car

In this chapter, let's explore:

♥ **The fact that it's okay to not get it right all of the time!**

♥ **What you can do to make things better when fear pops up.**

Even though I've known for some time that perfection doesn't exist, I sometimes forget and fall back into old familiar ways of thinking and behaving because, well, I'm not perfect!

Halfway through writing this book, I hit a roadblock. Little Miss Critical stepped right back onto my life's path and placed a big road sign in my way saying: "YOU NEED TO BE PERFECT!" This completely stopped me in my tracks. I had been doing so well. I had not heard from or seen Little Miss Critical in ages, and yet there she was, blocking my way again. I wasn't feeling perfect, but I wanted everything to be perfect. Was everything perfect? No. Did that mean I was a total failure? These were all the anxious and fearful thoughts running through my head.

It was a few days before my 22nd birthday—the first birthday

where I wouldn't have my family around to celebrate with me because they live in England and I now live 6,000 miles away in California. I was feeling homesick. I also couldn't find a dress to wear to my birthday celebration in any of the hundred-and-one shops I'd been searching through. I was starting to despair. I was no longer looking forward to my party because I felt like I didn't have anything special to wear—an insecurity that was exacerbated by how much I was missing my family.

It seemed that nothing was going right in my world. As I drove around town, going from shop to shop, stressing myself out and not fully acknowledging the emotions and anxiety I was feeling at being so far away from home, all my body issues resurfaced! Bam! There they were, handed to me on a silver platter by Little Miss Critical herself, and I didn't even know I had ordered anything in the first place.

I had just broken up with my boyfriend, I didn't know where my next acting job was coming from, and my mind was churning around and around with "what ifs": what if I couldn't pay my bills? What if I never landed another role? What if I let everyone down? What if? What if? What if? I felt disappointed and even ashamed of myself. I was symbolically towing a heavy trailer behind me that was piled full of my self-imposed expectations, worries, and fears, and my poor little Ford Focus was struggling to pull them any further!

I was feeling stuck, both physically and metaphorically. My back, neck, and shoulders were aching from all the stress I was placing on myself. I felt bloated and fat. I felt unworthy and very, very sad. Every time I went into yet another changing room trying to find a birthday dress, the more I just wanted to cry. I couldn't look at myself anymore.

At this point in my life, I had healed myself of an eating disorder and had learned to truly love the skin I'm in, and I was even writing a book about loving your body! How could these issues be resurfacing? The answer to that question was that I needed to remind myself that it's okay to not be perfect. I am on an exciting journey of loving myself exactly as I am with all my imperfections, and sometimes I need to remind myself of this. This was one of those times.

Because of all the expectations and stress I was piling onto myself, I had lost sight of just how far I had already come in my life. I had stopped appreciating myself and loving myself, I had forgotten about the commitments that I had made to the girl in the mirror, and I had opened up a space that allowed Little Miss Critical to get right back inside my head. Once she got in there, her negative chatter awakened Little Miss Fear.

Who is Little Miss Fear? She is the vulnerable, scared little girl who lives inside me who needs reassurance that I'm okay, that I'm safe, and that I'm going to survive. But I wasn't listening to her or reassuring her; I was too busy looking for a dress to wear to my party and feeling stressed out because I couldn't find it. The more I ignored Little Miss Fear, the louder she shouted and the more she demanded my attention until finally she took over altogether and started trying to drive my car! That was really scary.

I finally gave up my search for the perfect dress, pulled my car over to the side of the road, and allowed myself to cry. I let it all out. Full-on sobs! I cried out all the fearful feelings that were trapped inside of me. Afterwards, I realized that I didn't need a brand-new dress. My desperation at not finding one was simply a distraction from the love, attention, and acceptance that I wasn't giving myself. I was feeling fearful and anxious about this milestone in my life and I was homesick. I was scared that nobody would shower me with the same love and attention that family members usually give me on my birthday. I missed my mum.

So instead of driving frantically around the streets of Los Angeles in search of a dress, I decided to drive home and give some love and attention to the little girl inside of me who was feeling scared and lonely. I did a few rounds of tapping, using the "set-up" phrases

"Even though I'm feeling scared and lonely and I miss my mum, I love and accept myself completely."

and

"Even though I'm feeling fat and bloated, I love and accept myself completely."

That calmed me down. I ran myself a bath with lots of bubbles and lavender oil and had a long, luxurious soak while listening to some of my favorite music. Then I ate a delicious dinner and wrote in my journal about all the emotions I had been feeling and what it meant for me to be celebrating my birthday so far away from home. After I had let it all out, I watched one of my favorite chick-flick movies and got a great night's sleep.

Sometimes, all we need to do is spend a little time with ourselves and honor the emotions inside of us. The next day, I woke up feeling refreshed and light and like a brand-new person. I found a beautiful new pair of shoes to go with a dress I already had, and I felt so special wearing my sparkly new numbers at my party! I was actually glad I hadn't spent that money on a dress because the new shoes now go with all of my dresses. Some things are just meant to be, right?

We all have fearful voices inside of us that pop up for re-assurance from time to time, but ...

It is how we choose to respond to fearful thoughts and feelings that determines whether they take the driver's seat in our lives or not.

Many of us are scared of our emotions. We feel the need to run away from them; to pretend they don't exist; to put some imaginary earphones on to block out the noise. But just because the earphones are on, does it mean that the feelings go away? No. The feelings will shout louder and louder, like little children, until we listen to them and give them some attention.

You see, when I let Little Miss Critical back into my head telling me that I needed to be perfect when things just weren't, the little girl inside of me got really scared. She thought that her security and future wellbeing were under threat. But, instead of listening to her fears and reassuring her that she would be okay,

I first ignored her. I shut her out because I was too busy looking for a new dress to try to make myself look "perfect" for my party! The more I refused to listen, the more powerful her fear became until, finally, it sneaked right past me, plonked itself in the driver's seat, and took control of the car.

That made me pay attention!

Luckily, before it was too late, I realized I had lost control and took appropriate action to avoid a crash. My friend Kindness took over and showed me how to reassure Little Miss Fear. I focused on the frightened little girl inside of me. I listened to her fears and her worries about the future, and I reassured her that she didn't have to be perfect. I told her that I was so sorry that I had forgotten the commitment I had made to her. I reminded her that I really do love her exactly as she is, at where she is in her life at this moment, and regardless of what she wears to her party! I told her that she is beautiful exactly as she is and, no matter what the future brings, I will always be there for her and love her for the rest of her life. Then, without even having to be asked, Little Miss Fear hopped out of the driver's seat and into the back of the car and fell fast asleep immediately.

Let's face it: fear is a natural and even vital part of being a human being, isn't it? So let's accept that Little Miss Fear is going to be along for the ride, but as Elizabeth Gilbert says in her book *Big Magic*, we must make it absolutely clear that she will not be picking the music playlist, she cannot provide any of the road trip snacks, and she will not dictate the route we take. End of story.

Of course, there will be times on the journey where you will come across bumps in the road or feel like you're falling into old patterns. But don't sweat it—all is not lost! Now that you've got

Kindness, Positivity, and Gratitude on your side and a new way of dealing with things, you can jump over those bumps and feel even stronger after getting past them. This is where having your beautiful framed commitments from Chapter 4 really comes in handy! In times when we veer off course or Little Miss Critical creeps back in, look back and remember those empowering promises you made to yourself.

It's not the bumps in the road that determine how you are going to feel; it's how you choose to deal with them.

Chapter Summary

There will be times when old habits will resurface, especially when you are stressed and not listening to how you are feeling inside. Don't beat yourself up about it. Instead:

STOP.

Ask yourself how you are feeling.

Listen to what your body is telling you.

Do some tapping.

Be kind to yourself.

My smile is my favorite part of my body. I think a smile can make your whole body.

—*Serena Williams*

CHAPTER 9

Simple Ways to Appreciate Your Body Every Day

In this chapter, you'll learn:

♥ Simple ways to show your body some good ol' loving every day.

♥ The amazing benefits of dancing and moving your body.

♥ How to instantly turn your mood around.

♥ Much, much more!

Wow, we've talked about some pretty deep stuff so far. Because of this, I really wanted to also share with you some of the super fun and enjoyable ways that we can learn to love our bodies every single day. These are so easy to incorporate into your daily routine! Remember:

When you take care of your body and show it the love it deserves, your body will love you in return.

Dancing

In the words of Taylor Swift, let's shake it off!

Rarely in life do we allow ourselves to really let go. Most of us are too afraid of what other people will think of us if we just let ourselves relax, forget about everything for a few minutes, and dance crazily. I used to be so stuck in my body that I was too scared to even let myself go and dance in the privacy of my own room. Little Miss Critical would judge me and tell me I looked stupid. I can't tell you how liberating it is to finally be free of that limited way of thinking and feeling. Since I discovered the power of dance and expressing myself through movement, my body and mind have become so much happier and healthier.

As part of a week-long drama workshop I attended a few years back, we had to dance for an hour every morning. This was something I had never done before. I am not a dancer, and I have never been someone who could easily follow choreography. In fact, I'd always felt pretty self-conscious dancing. But, for this one hour, I decided to not let that matter.

We danced to a mixture of easy Latin and Zumba moves, and during the class I could literally feel my overly acute body-consciousness start to melt away as I began to truly let myself go. I didn't need to worry about the steps; I just let my body take me. After that first hour of dance, even though I was a sweaty mess, I felt so much more alive than before the class! I had begun to finally move my body in such a free and uninhibited way that my energy was really flowing and it was radiating out of me. I felt strong, powerful, and as if I could do anything because I was totally present in my body.

Through movement, I was now more aware of certain parts of my body; I felt loose and free and confident. It was like a form of therapy. I had been so tense because I had been holding onto so many negative thoughts towards my body, but when you're dancing, there's no room for that negativity. You *have* to let it go. And it feels incredible when you do.

That week, I danced for an hour every morning and I can truly say that, by the end of the week, I felt transformed. My energy was flowing freely and I saw a different body when I looked in the mirror. It is simply a brilliant way to feel alive! Not only is it great exercise, but there's something very healing about it, as well. And who cares if you aren't a brilliant dancer!? That's right: nobody.

You don't even have to go to a dance class if you don't want to or don't have access to one; what's great about dancing is that you can do it anywhere, anyhow, and to whatever music you like. You can do it in the privacy of your own room wearing earphones if you like. Make yourself a playlist of your favorite dance songs and just let the music take you. Don't worry about looking good or being "cool"—the wilder and crazier you get, the more effective it will be. Shock yourself. It's just you and the music. And, after you've been dancing for five minutes, I promise you'll feel happier and more positive than you did when you began.

What if you did this every morning before school for just a couple of minutes? Or before you go out to meet your friends? I guarantee you will feel so much more alive, confident, and happy in your own skin. The added bonus is that other people will be attracted to the radiance of your energy. It always makes me giggle when I head to the grocery store after my dance class or workout with my hair scraped back, not an ounce of makeup on, and sweat still dripping down my face and I have *more* people talk to me and interact with me in a friendly and happy way. Why? Because my energy is radiating out of me and I feel present and confident in my body. Happiness attracts positive people. Like attracts like.

Shake It, Gorgeous Girlie!

Here are a few of my favorite songs to shake to:

"Happy" by Pharell Williams

"Girls Just Want to Have Fun" by Cyndi Lauper

"Shake It Off" by Taylor Swift

"Love Myself" by Hailee Steinfeld

"Formation" by Beyoncé

"Diamonds" by Rihanna

"How Deep Is Your Love" by Calvin Harris

"'Firework" by Katy Perry

"Run the World" by Beyoncé

"Can't Hold Us Down" by Christina Aguilera and Lil' Kim

"Stronger" by Kelly Clarkson

"Move Your Body" by Sia

"Skyscraper" by Demi Lovato

"Fighter" by Christina Aguilera

"Alive" by Sia

Appreciate That Body!

Shower your body with love—literally and metaphorically.

When you're in the shower, imagine that the water pouring down over you is made from pure loving energy. Imagine it seeping happiness and appreciation deep into the core of your body. As you're washing yourself, give thanks for the amazing skin you're in and the power that lies beneath it. As you're doing that, remind your beautiful body how amazing it is by showering it with compliments, too. Again, this might feel silly when you first start doing it, but who cares? It's just for you!

Here are some to try out:

"I love my soft skin..."

"I love my arms because they allow me to hug the people I love..."

"I love my tummy. Thank you, tummy..."

"I love my beautiful, shiny hair."

"I'm blessed to have this body!"

"I love the skin I am in!"

When I get out of the shower, I always rub moisturizer into my skin. I take this time to nourish my body. Similarly, I say positive affirmations to myself as I rub the cream in and really take the time to appreciate my skin. We often don't take the time to take care of our bodies, but adding just a few minutes onto your routine to really appreciate the body you've been given can make such a big difference to how you feel. You don't even need to say it out loud if that makes you feel too self-conscious. Just take it one step at a time. Say the affirmations in your mind in a loving voice—even if you don't believe them at first—and notice how these loving thoughts soon become second nature.

If you're ever feeling run down or need some time off, know that it is okay to give yourself some tender loving care by resting and honoring what your body needs. I love to take a break by soaking in the bathtub and listening to music or reading a good book. Show your body that you care about it, and don't be afraid to take the time to love and appreciate it.

Write Yourself a Reminder or Memo!

Are you ever worried you'll forget something, so you write yourself a note to remember later? Something like, "Don't forget your keys!" or, "Remember Biology Book!" Well, what if you wrote yourself little reminders to love and appreciate yourself? Appreciating yourself and honoring who you are is way too important to forget to do. In act, remembering to be kind to yourself is probably one of the most important things you can remember to do in life.

I have little notes written on brightly colored paper up on my mirrors and around my home that fill me with positivity. You could frame beautiful, inspirational quotes, or just scribble your own memos and place them where you'll see them daily. Here are some of the reminders you could write for yourself:

Smile!

Do you know how awesome you are?

I love the skin I'm in!

You are beautiful inside and out.

Don't worry, Little Miss Fear, I've got this!

Today, I choose to let my light shine.

This is a great way to remind yourself to be happy. I've even placed reminders in places I've totally forgotten about, only to find them later when I most needed to hear it. Remember, it's not selfish to remind yourself of how awesome you are. And it certainly isn't big-headed; we've got that thinking all mixed up. It's actually the most loving thing you can do for yourself, your family, and for anyone you come into contact with. When you truly love and appreciate yourself, you will have plenty of love and appreciation to go around.

Write a Love Letter to Yourself!

Say what? A love letter? *To myself?* Yeah, okay, I know that sounds cheesy. But, honestly, it's not as whacky as it sounds. Why is it okay to think of someone else writing a love letter to us, but we find it so hard to imagine doing that for ourselves? Knowing your own worth and having confidence in who you are is the most beautiful accessory you could ever carry. Plus, it's contagious and magnetic.

I challenge you to write a love letter to yourself explaining all the things you really admire and appreciate about yourself. I know this may seem really weird, but it's for your eyes only and not to be shared with anyone else. There are so many wonderful things that make you an amazing and unique person, but it's also easy to take these things for granted or overlook them. It may even seem weird while you're writing it, but I bet you that your energy towards yourself will be so different once you step away from that letter and look at it with fresh eyes.

Try starting out with:

"Dear Body, have I told you lately that I love you?"

When you're finished, I recommend putting it somewhere safe, and when you're feeling a bit low, take it out and read it to remind yourself of all the wonderful things you have going on! This doesn't make you big-headed or self-obsessed. It's about loving and accepting who you are from within and having a secret inner confidence that radiates silently outwards.

Chapter Summary

In this chapter, you have:

♥ **Become ready to shake it off and unleash your confident and loving self by throwing some moves to your favorite tunes!**

♥ **Remembered to be present in your private moments so you can remind your body of how awesome it is.**

♥ **Created some fun memos for yourself that should put a smile on your face every time you see them.**

♥ **Grabbed a pen and paper and written a loving and appreciative letter to yourself!**

Do you feel powerful? Energized? A little silly? Good! You're so ready to take on the awesome responsibility of loving yourself for who you are. I can feel it.

I wish I could tell every young girl that she's worthy of life and that her life has meaning. You can overcome and get through anything.

—Demi Lovato

CHAPTER 10

You Can Do This!

Wow, you've made it all the way through the book, and I am so proud of you. What an incredible journey we've been on together. I know it can be tough to face your fears head-on, but look at how brave you've been! Acknowledging your fears and then pushing through them makes you infinitely more powerful that you could ever imagine. And now that you have the tools to break through your body barriers, the world is your oyster, girlfriend. You might have to focus on one day at a time—sometimes even just one minute. There may be setbacks, just like I had. But no matter what, know this: you deserve to love your body. It's your right. And nobody should ever be able to take that away from you— especially not your own Little Miss C.

Loving the girl in the mirror is a gift you have to bestow upon yourself. It's been the most amazing gift I have ever received. When you value your body and your being, you allow other people to value you at that high level, too. It'll have a snowball effect on your relationships, your confidence levels, how you feel in social situations, and even how you feel and are treated later on in the workplace, too. When you respect your incredible body and treat it with love and adoration, just watch how the world opens up to you with the same devotion and respect!

So, now that you've finished reading *Learning to Love the Girl in the Mirror*, let's take a quick moment to summarize the nine key things that you can do to move closer towards a happy, healthy mind and body that oozes self-love and confidence.

1. Say Goodbye to Little Miss Critical

Thank her for trying her best to keep you safe, but let her know that you're now ready to take back the reins of your own life. Tell her to pack her bags and send her off on a lifelong vacation.

2. Make Best Friends with the Girl in the Mirror

Every day, tell yourself three things that you appreciate and admire about yourself when you look in the mirror.

3. Listen to Your Fears, But Don't Let Them Dictate Your Choices

Don't be afraid to acknowledge your feelings and let them out. Just don't let Little Miss Fear anywhere near the steering wheel of your life!

4. Use My Top Five Stress-Busters

Teenage life is full of stressors, and stress plays a major role in the development of unhealthy eating habits and disorders. Find positive ways to release and manage your stress and make time to cherish yourself.

5. Love the Foods You Eat

Learn to love and enjoy the foods you eat by nourishing your body with top-quality fuel.

6. Show Appreciation to Your Body

Literally shower yourself with compliments by taking time for yourself in the shower and appreciating and being loving to your body as you get dressed every morning.

7. Write Yourself a Love Letter

Tell yourself all the lovely things you would like someone else to write to you. Keep it, cherish it, and read it anytime you need to be reminded of how wonderful, unique, and special you are!

8. Dance!

Release stress and let go of the tension and blockages in your energy system by dancing wildly and uninhibitedly, either in a class or in the privacy of your own bedroom. I do it throughout the week and I'm so much happier for it!

9. Tap into your fullest potential

Use the tapping technique to release any blocked energy in your body and to reprogram any negative and destructive thoughts that are standing in your way of showing up as the best, most confident, and happiest version of you.

Every single tool that's here in this book has the power to change how you feel about yourself for the rest of your life. You are too special to allow unnecessary and misguided feelings about yourself to hold you back from sharing your incredible gifts with the world. Let this book be a go-to source of comfort and support when the road gets rocky— along with trusted family, friends, and medical professionals, if appropriate. Go back and re-read the chapters that most resonated with you. When you feel confused or sense Little Miss Critical starting to sneak back in, pick up this toolkit and show her who's in charge!

You've so got this, girl. I believe in you.

Another great way to stay empowered and feel supported during your journey is by joining our Girl Unfiltered community for daily doses of kickass inspiration. It's a great way to connect with other like-minded girls who are on the same journey as you.

Remember, gorgeous girlie, you are never alone in this. We are all in it together.

[O] @girl_unfiltered

Lastly, head over to the website and join the Girl Unfiltered gang!

www.girlunfiltered.com

Acknowledgements

There are many people in my life who have influenced me in becoming the woman I am today; some without even realizing it.

I want to thank my family for always supporting me and for allowing me to believe in the beauty of my dreams.

Mum, thank you for being my rock. Without you, I would never have written this book, and I am so thankful for everything that has brought us to where we are today. You really are a best friend as well as my beautiful mother.

Dad, I am so proud to have you as my father, even if you do insist on still wearing clothes that are older than me! I give you permission to continue to embarrass me as much as you like, because secretly I like it! I always feel your presence looking out for me, even if I do live 6,000 miles away. Mum and Dad, I love you both so much. Thank you for giving me my roots and then handing me my wings.

Auntie Lorraine, you continue to teach me what it means to be a woman who can kick ass and stand up for herself in any situation. Thank you for the love you shower me with.

Thank you to the best friends a girl could ever ask for: Alice, Olivia, Tara, and Kate. My cheerleaders from all corners of the world!

Huge thanks to Barbara Donoghue for your invaluable feedback and advice in the early stages of writing. You helped me to structure my "stream of consciousness" into the book it became. I am so grateful.

Many thanks to the amazing teen girls who took the time to read early drafts and give me amazing feedback. It all helped so much!

And thank you to all of you who believed in me before I was even capable of believing in myself. Every kind word of encouragement continues to play a huge part in my journey.

Resources

Hey, gorgeous girlie, if you ever feel that you need to talk to somebody or seek professional help, then I urge you to do so. Asking for help is never a sign of weakness; it is a sign of strength and maturity, and I wish I had done it sooner.

You might like to start by talking to your parents or to other trusted adults, such as a school counselor, teacher, or doctor.

Below is also a list of hotlines and professionals that can offer help and support for a variety of things. If I haven't listed one in your area, please do some research online and see if there's one closer to you or one that feels more appropriate for you and your needs. Remember, you're not alone, and there are people who want to help you!

Specialized Support via Skype From Anywhere In The World:

For personal support from a coach who specializes in empowering girls, visit www.empoweringgirlswitheft.com

(She also specializes in the tapping technique we used in Chapter 7!)

Hotlines

Based in the USA:

National Eating Disorders Association (NEDA)

https://www.nationaleatingdisorders.org/

Call 1-800-931-2237 Monday to Thursday 9:00am – 9:00pm and Friday from 9:00am – 5:00pm (EST). In a crisis, please text "NEDA" to 741741 to be connected to a trained volunteer.

Based in the UK:

Beating Eating Disorders (b-eat)

https://www.b-eat.co.uk/

Call 0845-634-7650 Monday – Friday 1:30 p.m. to 4:30 p.m., Mondays and Wednesdays 5:30 p.m. to 8:30 p.m.

Anorexia & Bulimia Care

National charity offering helplines, 1:2:1 befriending support, and nutrition guidance

http://www.anorexiabulimiacare.org.uk

Based in Ireland:

BodyWhys: The Eating Disorders Association of Ireland

www.bodywhys.ie

Call 1890-200-444. Their line is open for two hours every day, so check out the website for more details.

Based in Australia:

Eating Disorders Victoria

http://www.eatingdisorders.org.au

Call their helpline at 1300 550 236 or (03) 9417 6598 Monday to Friday from 9:30 a.m. – 5:00 p.m. If you call after hours, leave a message and they will return your call. You can also email them at help@eatingdisorders.org.au.

Based in Canada

The National Eating Disorder Information Centre (NEDIC)

Call Toll Free 1-866-633-4220 or Toronto 416-340-41560

www.nedic.ca

Based in New Zealand

www.ed.org.nz

Crisis 24-hour Answer Services 0800 800 717

About the Author

Helena Grace Donald is the founder of Girl Unfiltered. Her mission is to teach girls the value of self-love and self-acceptance so that they feel empowered as they journey into the wonderful world of womanhood. Still in her early twenties, Helena relates easily to teenage girls and truly understands what it feels like to be in their shoes. She grew up in England and currently lives in Los Angeles, where she leads a happy and creative life—acting, writing and raising awareness through public speaking engagements. She can be found through her web site at www.girlunfiltered.com.